THE CLEARANCE

THE CLEARANCE

JOAN LINGARD

HEINEMANN
NEW WINDMILLS

Heinemann Educational Books Ltd
Halley Court, Jordan Hill, Oxford OX2 8EJ
OXFORD   LONDON   EDINBURGH
MELBOURNE   SYDNEY   AUCKLAND
IBADAN   NAIROBI   GABORONE
KINGSTON   PORTSMOUTH NH (USA)
SINGAPORE   MADRID

ISBN 0 435 12228 2

The front cover shows Kirsty Miller as Maggie in the BBC
Television production *Maggie*.
Cover photograph © British Broadcasting Corporation 1983

For *Francine*
and her children

Printed and bound in Great Britain by
Richard Clay Ltd, Bungay, Suffolk

PART I
The Clearance

Chapter I

It was July. The midges were out, swarming under the trees, zinging like crazy, and scudding round my body looking for juicy spots. I scratched my waist feverishly, feeling that I could easily tear my skin to bits. I hated the country. Being there was like doing penance.

There is a glen in Inverness-shire. My granny's glen. At least it was, until that summer.

I had gone up to spend the school holidays with her; or rather, I had been drafted. Fond as I was of my granny, it would have taken a lot to make me volunteer to spend seven weeks in the backwoods.

My grandfather had been a forester. He lived in a Forestry Commission house in the glen, a black timbered building with a red corrugated iron roof, two rooms up, two down, and the loo in the back garden. No electricity either. You wouldn't catch me putting up with a place like that but I suppose they had no choice. Whereas I do. Granny met Grandpa when she was eighteen, a pretty brown-haired girl, living further up the glen. He courted her for seven years before they married. The patience of it! My mind boggles at the thought of letting seven years slip by, just waiting. I could understand the midges better, zooming around looking for action. Granny and

Grandpa had seven children, to keep and clothe and feed in that small house. My father was the youngest. He was a big strong lad, the spitting image of his father, according to Granny, but in looks alone it seems, for he had no notion to be a forester and spend his life in the wilds of Inverness-shire, and I didn't blame him.

He went to Glasgow where he got a job as a plumber's mate and married my mother who was city born and bred, and whose dad worked as a welder in the Clyde shipyards. My mother and father had three children— I'm in the middle—and we all live in a nice big flat in a block of sandstone tenements not far from the centre of the town. They're pulling half of Glasgow down; streets and streets of houses have crumpled under the demolition machines. We've stood and watched them, Sandy and Jean and I, with the dust puffing round us making us look like old grey-haired folk. It makes you feel funny inside to see rooms sliced down the middle, standing open to the wind, wallpaper flapping; places where people have lived. But it's not Glasgow I'm telling you about: it's my granny's glen.

I stood there on that July day leaning on the worm-eaten gate post, scratching my bites and looking up the glen. There wasn't much to see, mostly hills which blocked the sky so that you couldn't see all that far, a few trees, heather—miles of it—and the odd cow and sheep. Round the bend of the road, out of sight, was a farm, a big square house with a shelter belt of trees to protect it from the wind. You'd need more than a belt of trees up there in winter! Sometimes I went along to the farm but the man didn't talk much, he just went on milking his cows and grunting, and his wife was as deaf as the post I was leaning on. You couldn't exactly say the place was jumping.

On the other side of the road, opposite from my granny's house, was the old school and schoolhouse where my father had been educated. When he was a boy there were forty pupils; you would hardly believe it but my granny says they came from the whole length of the glen, trudging the road every morning and afternoon, laughing and shouting. It must have been livelier then, right enough, but even so it wouldn't have suited me, especially during the long dark months of winter.

Forty years ago, forty pupils; ten years ago, three. And then they closed the school and sold it to a man from Edinburgh who made it into a holiday house for his family, with running water, electricity, the lot. So there they were sitting across the road with their fridge, electric cooker and flush toilet, whilst my granny was on the other side carrying water and fumbling with an oil lamp. Makes you wonder. Makes you a bit mad too. Not my granny though.

"You can't look at things that way, Maggie," she said. "It's just the way things fall out in life. I don't mind. It's not their fault." I minded for her though. "Don't be sour now," she told me. "It'll no do you any good."

But they annoyed me, the Frasers, the smug way they trotted up and down the glen in sensible walking shoes, carrying rucksacks, with their chins up. "We're off to the hills, Mrs McKinley," they called out as they passed, and favoured us with a smile. Mr and Mrs are both teachers. You could tell from the way they spoke to you, nodding understandingly, asking sensible questions, and they smiled at you as if you were an idiot or slightly sub-

9

normal. He teaches history in a secondary school so was full of bits of information about the district; she teaches Infants and was forever cutting out things for friezes and collecting old bottle tops and toilet roll middles. James, that summer, was seventeen, tall, with floppy blond hair, and he wanted to be a doctor. His sister Catriona, who is a year younger, and the same age as me, was tall and blond too, and walked as if she was a model, or tried to, as far as the rucksack would let her. That was all I knew about them then.

I heard something moving behind me and looked round to see Granny coming out of her house. She hobbled towards me in big black boots, men's boots, for her feet were swollen with arthritis and she could get nothing else to fit them. She was eighty-three. She told everyone who passed and everyone said she didn't look anything like it but I thought she did, every bit of it, with her poor back bent and stooped, worn knotted hands, and face creased and scored like a gully. I hope I never live to be eighty-three.

She had lived alone for the past ten years, since my grandfather had died; and every now and then my father or one of his brothers or sisters would feel guilty and send one of their children up to keep her company for a while. "You never go," I said to my father when he told me I was to spend my summer holiday up there.

"I'm too busy," he said "and I only get two weeks off in the year." He likes to spend them at Rothesay or Dunoon, seaside resorts on the Clyde, or Scarborough, which is where he and my mother went that year.

Granny leant on the gate beside me. She wore a greyish, blue-flowered overall over an ancient grey jumper and skirt that met the top of her boots. I could never remember seeing her without that overall, except when she was going to bed when she took off the top layer of clothes and put on an old flannelette nightdress on top of her underclothes. My mother had told me to try to get her to change her underclothes more often, but how can you tell a granny of eighty-three to put on clean knickers? My mother's full of instructions that aren't all that easy to carry out. She can be nippy and sharp when it comes up her back, but if she was to have been sharp with Granny McKinley then Granny would just have pretended she hadn't heard. I decided anyway that it was unlikely anyone was going to change her habits after eighty-three years.

"It's a braw sky," said Granny. "Look, Maggie, look up over the hills!"

The sky was streaked pink and pale green, and shot with gold. Below, the hills were tinged with reflected pink light, making them look warm and soft and friendly, instead of hard and cold as they were on a grey day.

"The sky's aye changing," said Granny. "And the hills with it."

"It's bonny," I admitted, for, in spite of my prejudice against the glen, the colours got me.

"I never tire of watching, no matter the day or the weather."

"Never, Gran?"

"Never." She sounded very sure.

"Haven't you ever wanted to get away from the glen?"

"Get away? Whatever for?"

"There's so many things in the world."

"I've enough here."

"But it's lonely. All those cottages empty up the glen . . . " I shuddered. The sight of those abandoned, weed-clogged cottages, gradually crumbling and falling apart, year by year, some open to the sky, only the broken walls remaining, made me feel cold. A few of them had been gutted at the time of the Highland Clearances. That's way back in the nineteenth century when the crofters were driven out by the big landlords who wanted the land for sheep. Sutherland took the brunt of it but Ross-shire and Inverness-shire suffered too. The landlords, or rather their factors, who did their dirty work for them, drove out the people and burned down their houses so that they wouldn't try to go back.

"Mind you, Gran," I said, "I can't see why those folk made all that fuss about going. When they got their marching orders, I mean. They might have found something better."

My granny turned so fiercely I thought she'd eat the head off me. "You wouldn't fancy having your house in Glasgow pulled down would you?"

"Well no . . . " She had a point of course, and one man's meat is another man's poison, as my mother's overfond of saying, even though she doesn't believe a word of it and thinks that anyone who doesn't agree with her is off his head.

Granny was grunting and grumbling, all upset now because I'd said that.

"Sorry, Gran. I didn't think."

"That's the trouble with you at times, Maggie!" She looked at me. "My own granny was evicted. She was only a lassie at the time, eighteen years old."

"You've never told me."

"No. But I'll tell you now. Her name was Margaret Ross."

And this is the story she told me.

Margaret Ross lived with her sister Agnes on the estate of Greenyards in Strathcarron in Ross-shire. Their parents died when they were small and they were brought up by relatives. There were dozens of them in the glen. All Rosses.

Now in 1854, Margaret was eighteen years old, Agnes seventeen. They were a couple of bonny looking lasses, with plenty of spirit about them. On the 31st of March, as dawn was breaking, a band of policemen with the Sheriff at their head, entered the glen. They were carrying firearms, truncheons and eviction orders for the Rosses. They had sneaked over the hills in carts during the night and they'd had a good booze up to themselves whilst they were at it. So a number of them were a bit the worse for wear by the time they arrived.

They thought they had nothing else to do but march up the glen and hand out the notices, but they hadn't bargained on the Ross women. About four miles up the glen they found the road blocked by sixty or seventy of them wearing red shawls over their heads. It must have been a fine looking sight! A few men stood behind them, but not many. Not enough. Shame on those men of Ross. If I'd got my hands on them! The Sheriff called out to the women to get out of the way but they weren't going to pay any attention to the likes of him. They stared back at him, and not an inch did they budge.

The Sheriff was mad. He ordered his men to knock them down. They were only too pleased to lay into the women; they'd been dying for the chance. They clubbed them, pulled them along the road by their hair, broke their arms. Most of the men ran for the hills.

It was a vicious and bloody attack, one of the worst in the Clearances. When it was over blood lay in pools on the ground on the banks of the river Carron. The grass and earth were red from the women's blood, and dogs came to lick it up. Even after the women had fallen the policemen went on beating them like maniacs. Some were hand-cuffed together, others tied up with ropes like animals, and taken in carts to the jail in Tain. And all because they didn't want to be put out of their own homes!

Margaret Ross was cut and bruised but Agnes came off worse, with a broken head and arm. Margaret dragged her sister clear of the disaster area and they lay under bushes until the trouble was over and night came. Margaret bathed Agnes's wounds with water from the river and bound them with strips torn from her petticoat. They didn't want to go back to their cottage to await eviction, so they set off southwards.

They staggered on for days, not knowing where they were heading, not caring probably, just wanting to get away from the glen and the blood on the riverbank. Crofters with anything to spare gave them scraps of food. Agnes, who had lost a lot of blood, got weaker and weaker, and for a good bit of the time Margaret had to carry her over her back, like a bag of potatoes.

They crossed into Inverness-shire, without knowing it, I suppose, and at last came to this glen where Agnes keeled right over. Margaret ran to the nearest cottage and hammered on the door. A young man opened it. His name was James Grant and he lived with his old mother.

They carried Agnes in, he and Margaret between them. There wasn't much life in her, she'd lost so much blood, and in the morning she died, with the two of them beside her. Margaret stayed for she fancied James and he fancied her, and soon they were married, all set to live happily ever after. And it seems they did too. They had a son who, when he married, had a daughter. He called the daughter Margaret after his mother. And that Margaret was my granny.

I was quiet after Granny finished her story. So was she. Her eyes had a kind of far-away look.

"She was a fine woman, my granny," she said. "I mind her sitting by the fire telling me the story, and others forby."

"She was a brave girl," I said, fired by visions of her fighting off police and carrying her sister on her back through rain and mist. I was glad she'd had a bit of luck at the end of it. Granny looked back up the glen. "I'm thankful the place hasn't gone like some glens, all choked up with cars and folk."

A few tourists came here, but not many, and they were the serious, country-loving ones who roamed the hills, collected wild flowers in plastic bags, watched birds, and dropped no litter. The glen was not spectacular enough to attract tourists in the mass: it had no loch or big river, only a small twisting burn, the hills were not particularly high or splendid, and further up, at the head of the glen, the moors began, bare and brown and barren.

The sky was changing every minute, deepening and darkening, the pink changing to red, the green to peacock and grey. You couldn't take your eyes off it for a minute; if you did you looked back and found you'd missed something. I hate missing things. "You've eyes and ears as sharp as tacks," my mother tells me, but meaning of course that I pick up a lot of things she'd rather I didn't.

"It's a fine sky," said Granny, nodding at it. "That makes it worth it."

Now it was a fine sight, I've already admitted that, though Granny would have liked me to say the same thing over and over again, as she did; but you can't live on sunsets alone, and I'd have enjoyed the sunset in the street at home just as much, probably better, for after the sun would go and leave the world grey there would be brightly lit rooms to go into and friends to blether with. Here we would go inside and when you couldn't see your finger in front of your nose Granny would light the paraffin lamp and we would sit with it flickering round us casting ghostly shadows on the walls, and Granny would nod off to sleep with her chin sunk down on her chest, and I would huddle by the lamp and read. Six more weeks of that! The thought was enough to drive me up the wall.

"Wouldn't you like to come and live with us in Glasgow, Gran?"

"Glasgow?" It might have been the Chamber of Horrors the way she said it. "I hate the place."

"You've never been."

"I don't need to. I've heard. Dirty streets, no space for folk to breathe in. I never understood why your dad went."

All her family were gone: two had died, the rest had found work in Glasgow, Dundee, England or Canada,

16

like the inhabitants of the empty cottages. One son had set himself up as a hairdresser in London and was doing well. Hairdresser! London! No good would come of that, his mother had predicted. She had been waiting forty years for bad news of him.

"Don't you like seeing people, Gran?"

"The grocer calls on Friday and there's the folk at the farm. And then the Frasers are here in the summer."

"The Frasers!" I said with contempt.

At that moment, bang on cue, they came round the corner. Maggie McKinley, you have a way with timing!

Chapter II

The Frasers had heard me saying their name but were too polite to show it. James and Catriona walked ahead of their parents; they walked in an easy kind of way, swinging their arms, heads up, as if the world belonged to them. Their cheeks shone. Anybody's face would get a shine after a day of sun and wind up in those hills, but if I was to go up I'd come down with windburn or a rash. As I straightened myself up from the post and looked at those ruddy examples of good health, I felt sallow, all over. I've got skin like a Chinaman, my mother says; I'd need to go for a walk in the face of a Force Ten gale before I'd get even a nip of pink in my cheeks. Peely-wally, we call it in Scotland. That's me: Peely-Wally Maggie. Before I go to a dance I stand in front of the mirror for hours pinching the skin over my cheekbones.

The Frasers halted in front of us, a bit like an army platoon. Hup, two, three, four, at ease!

"Lovely evening, Mrs McKinley," said Mr Fraser.

"Aye, it's real braw."

"Hello, Maggie," said Mrs Fraser, all dimples in her plump cheeks. She smiled nearly all the time, much more than my mother, but then Mrs Fraser's had more to smile about. My mother's had to work like a Trojan since the day she was fourteen (she's always telling me, when I'm sitting reading or lying in bed); she started in the packing department of a cotton thread company, moved on to the looms, cleaned other folk's houses after we kids were born, even took in washing in hard times. I wouldn't have to do any of those things because I had that magic thing—education!

The Frasers didn't think I had, the way they smiled at me.

I said hello to Mrs Fraser, almost cracking my face in the effort to smile back. My granny was always giving me a row about not being nice to them. But I didn't feel nice.

"Hi!" said James, pushing a piece of that blond hair back from his forehead. The skin looked damp under the hair. They must have walked for miles. And on such a hot day! When they talked about the miles they did they seemed to imply that virtue went hand in hand with physical exertion. Round the pitch now, girls, one more time! Come on, tackle, Maggie, tackle! Oh, those nasty hockey sticks and hard balls and puffing girls! None of that's in my line. I'm ill as often as possible when it's time for any form of physical education.

I nodded at James and wished I could have said "Hi!" back as coolly as I would if I'd met a boy in the street at home. James was a nice-looking boy and if my friend Isobel had been here she'd have been chatting him up and flapping her purple eyelashes at him. Or maybe she wouldn't, not in this glen, for the quietness did things to you.

"We walked right along the ridge," said Catriona in her lofty Edinburgh voice that made me want to talk as broadly Glaswegian as I could. All terribly infantile.

"I mind the day when I did that myself," said Granny. "But as far as the bend in the road's my limit now."

They all began to protest how marvellous she was and they only hoped they'd be half as fit at her age. I stuck my hands in the pockets of my jeans and tried to elevate myself; I eased my heels up on to a little bump of ground, wishing I was three inches taller so that I could have looked Catriona Fraser straight in the eye. Or four, so that I could have looked down on her.

"Have you ever been up on the ridge, Maggie?" asked Mr Fraser.

"Me?" I jumped, for I hadn't been following their conversation. "Up there? No. Never."

"Never?" Catriona seemed astounded.

"I don't like hills," I said, shocking the Frasers, as I knew I would. To them the hills were sacred; they plodded up and down them as purposefully and reverently as pilgrims trudging to Mecca. It's a form of religion. Like Bingo, or football. My mother goes to Bingo; Mrs Fraser takes to the hills. "I don't have to like them, do I?" I asked. I seemed to have struck them dumb. It was the first time that I hadn't heard them chattering. I no longer felt awkward; I was enjoying myself.

"She's a city lass," said Granny apologetically.

"But you'd think—" began Mrs Fraser. "Well, I mean, having you here . . . and her father born here."

"He hates hills too," I said. "He likes the football on a Saturday. Hampden Park, and the crowd cheering." I didn't know if he did or not; he goes to the football but he never comes home exactly ecstatic. He sits and grumbles in his chair if his team gets beaten; if they win, he'll go so far as to say, "They're no bad this season." I couldn't imagine him going mad on the terraces but then how did I know? I was so carried away by the vision of my father jumping up and down swinging a rattle that I almost forgot the Frasers. They were waiting for me to continue. "Hills or streets?" I said. "You're no better if you like one more than the other are you?"

"Of course not, Maggie," said Mrs Fraser, but she was not convinced, I could see that. To her the hills would always win, hands down. It was all to do with fresh air and exercise and lack of people.

"I don't see why she has to like hills," said James. As Granny often said, he was a nice lad. I smiled at him, I couldn't help it. "It's all a matter of taste, isn't it?" he went on.

His sister didn't like him for saying it. "But city streets are polluted," she protested, reminding me of the two minute talks we give at school. "They're noisy and busy—"

"Great!" I said. "I love it when it's all go."

"Yes, James, you're right," said his mother. "We mustn't make a virtue out of our own pleasures."

"This is a lovely part of the world anyway," said Mr Fraser. "And we're glad that we're part-time inhabitants at least."

Granny was muttering inaudibly under her breath but I had a fair idea of what she might be saying. Mrs Fraser said to her that she must go and feed her hungry mob, and then she turned to me.

"Why don't you come over later, dear, and play records with Catriona and James?"

"Yes, do," said James. "That would be nice."

"Thanks all the same," I said "but I've got to write to my mother."

"You can do that in the morn," said Granny, who had asked me every day since I'd come when I was going to write home.

I said that I wanted to give it to the postman in the morning, all prunes and prisms and oh, so righteous! The trouble is righteousness never gives me much of a kick. I get two minutes' satisfaction and spend the rest of the day suffering.

"Perhaps another time then," said Mrs Fraser.

They moved off, their tongues clacking again. You could hear them from the moment they opened the door in the morning. My family doesn't do all that much talking. I make up for them, my mother says. I talk at them, testing theories, putting opposing points of view, asking at the end, "What do you think then?" knowing they won't have thought anything since they haven't been listening. My father's usually studying the racing form, my mother's watching telly, Sandy has his ear permanently glued to his transistor and Jean has her nose in *True Love* or something equally elevating. I don't mean to run them down. They drive me nuts but they're O.K., on the whole. And I expect there'll come a day when Sandy takes his ear off and Jean lifts her nose. My parents I've given up on of course.

"But it's not just a matter of fresh air," Catriona was saying as they crossed the road. "There's the question of violence. Crowded places breed—"

They went inside.

Catriona had a few notions I could have set her straight on. The whole of Glasgow's not filled with gangs; there's ordinary folk walking about too, not killing each other, just getting on with their lives, doing the best they can.

"You're a right cussed lassie," said Granny. "And I don't know why you didn't say you'd go when they asked you. You're needing some young company."

"Ach, Gran, the Frasers were just patronising me."

"Patronising you?"

"They don't think I'm as good as them. They feel sorry for me."

"You're havering. They've no side to them."

What my granny meant was: the Frasers are better class than us (she still puts people into classes, like a lot of others who won't admit it) but they're nice to us and they don't treat us as if we were inferior. She was always a great one for recognising her 'position'. More trouble came from not keeping to it, she claimed. We had a few arguments about that but never got anywhere, so I let her remark go now. I took her arm and we went inside.

A fire crackled in the old black range, and the kettle steamed on the hob. Granny made tea in a brown enamelled teapot that was almost as old and dented as herself. I once bought her a shiny new one but there it sat on the shelf, as bright and unstained as the day it left the shop.

We sat on either side of the fire with a rickety card-table between us. We drank thick dark tea and ate thick stale bread that had been bought from the grocer's van the Friday before. That's another thing I couldn't take about that kind of life: the lack of fresh food. I like to run out to the shop for soft fresh rolls in the morning and come back feeling the warmth of them against me. But in

23

spite of the staleness, I ate like a starved wolf, devouring slice after slice with butter and cheese and jam. I have a huge appetite, though you wouldn't think it from the skinniness of me. My mother says I burn it up 'with all that thinking'. My family aren't too sure about all that thinking and reading and writing. Oh they approve, and they're pleased that their Maggie is smart and won't end up standing behind a shop counter or scrubbing floors, but they're a wee bit uneasy all the same.

After supper Granny lit the lamp, for it was almost dark in the low room although there was still a lot of light left outside. On July evenings it's seldom all that dark up there. I watched her hands trimming the lamp, the fingers, though knotted and bent, moving deftly. She had done it so many times.

"Do you remember the first time you trimmed the lamp, Granny, in this house?"

She looked up, remembering, and her eyes went all soft. I could see a bit of what she was sixty years ago. If I half closed my eyes I could imagine a tall bonny girl with brown hair sitting there.

"Aye, I mind fine. I made a right mess of it, I was that nervous!" She chuckled.

"You nervous?"

"Oh I was wanting to make Andrew a good wife and do everything the right way, but you see, Maggie, I wasn't very fond of the domestic life. That was why I'd swithered as long. I'd have liked better to work as a forester myself and planted trees and looked after them as they were coming up." The lamp was lit now; she set it on the table. "But I'm no complaining. Lassies hadn't any choice then and Andrew was a good husband to me."

24

She went on to tell me what a handsome lad he was, how all the girls used to eye him at the *ceilidhes* and would jump to make a third with him and Granny for the *Dashing White Sergeant*. He never asked anyone but Granny to dance of course. And Jess Gordon from the braehead never forgave her for getting Andrew McKinley; she kept a spite for her till the day she died.

Then out came the photographs, brown and faded, cracked and fingered. I had seen them thousands of times, from as early as I could remember, but I enjoyed looking again and asking, "Who's that, Granny?"

After a bit she grew tired, her hands slipped on the photographs and they dropped into her lap. I packed the photographs away in the old chocolate box with the picture of a large red rose on the lid, then I put the box up on the shelf beside the tea caddy.

I filled the kettle to heat water for the dishes. I washed them in an enamelled basin, white with a blue rim, well chipped round the edges, but as much a part of my Granny as her teapot and kettle. "You get fond of the old things," she said, and was not tempted by bright shiny plastic. Bright colours were not for her; she couldn't feel at home with scarlet or canary yellow. Colours I love. They make me sing inside.

By the time I had dried the last spoon her chin was sinking on to her overall. I hoped she was dreaming of Andrew, of dancing with him at the *ceilidh*, and laughing.

I carried the dirty water out into the garden. The smell of the undergrowth hit me. I took in a big lungful of the night air. It was sweet, right enough, and I felt it going to my head in the same way that a glass of my father's port had done one Hogmanay. The sky was a dark indigo, with little slivers of pink and gold still showing. Every now and then the place did catch hold of me, made me stop dead like this, and wonder. And that moment I felt, in a funny way, part of it, even though while I was feeling it I knew it wouldn't last.

Water slopping from the basin on to my feet broke the trance. I carried it over by the fence and tipped the rest of the dirty water there, where the nettles grew strong and tall. No flowers bloomed in this garden, at least no cultivated ones, only a few wild ones whose names I never remember; but for the most part it was a wilderness, a piece of ground overgrown with weeds. Granny could no longer work it.

"Granny McKinley's a worry to us," my mother said often. "She'll no come to Glasgow and she won't go into a home." They had tried to persuade her several times but she would not be budged from the glen, and as my father said, "You can't carry her out bodily." Well, you could, but we hadn't thought it would come to that.

As I turned to go back indoors I saw someone come out of the house across the road. It was James. He raised his hand to me, a ghostly shadow in the half-dark, and I raised my free one, just a little, to let him know that I'd seen him.

The evening was still warm. We didn't need a fire but Granny must light one every day. The windows were all stuck so I left the front door open. I sat beside the window in the circle of yellow cast by the lamp and wrote a letter to my mother. I couldn't think of much to say, now that I was sitting down to it, and I was feeling lazy too, what with the warmth and smell of the burning pine logs, and the closeness of the room that not even an open door could break, as well as the sleepiness that comes over you after a long day in the fresh air. So I yawned and scribbled a little and doodled and from time to time lifted my head to look at the lighted windows across the road. They must have had their windows open too for I could hear music, and once or twice the sound of laughter.

Granny woke up with a start and said, "Well, I think I'll be off to my bed. I can't keep my eyes open."

We doused the fire and I carried the lamp upstairs. The stairs were steep and she could only just manage them but she wouldn't listen when I suggested she slept downstairs. She liked going up to bed, and as long as her legs would carry her she would do it. I could understand that. Cussed she was, just like my father.

It was even stuffier in the two small rooms under the tin roof but I could at least open a window. I had forced it apart the night I arrived, unable to stand the lack of air. Granny, for all her delight in fresh country air, slept nightly without any. Night air was bad, she told me, and she was eighty-three so she should know.

The music was still there when I drifted off into sleep. I dreamt. I dreamt that Mr Fraser was the teacher at the school across the road. The bell was ringing and children were running along the road, converging on the school from both directions, calling to one another and swinging their satchels. They wore big laced up boots, smaller versions of my granny's, and heavy dark clothes. I was standing by the gate post watching them as they filed into school. Then, when the road had quietened, I looked round and saw James coming towards me. He was wearing a leather jerkin and knee breeches. My mind had slipped backwards in time.

Chapter III

I awoke thinking of my granny and grandpa. Had I been dreaming about them? I crossed to the window, feeling the rough wooden boards snagging my bare feet, and leaned out, half expecting to see her, in a long tweed skirt and a shawl gathered about her shoulders, waiting by the gate for her strong forester husband to come along the road, his brown face breaking into a smile as he saw her. But the road was empty. And then I remembered it was James Fraser who had been in my dream.

The Frasers' house still slept, curtains drawn tight against the morning sun. Not a sound, not a movement. It pleased me to watch their house and know that they slept unaware that I watched.

It was just six o'clock. A slight mist hovered over the fields but soon it would be chased away by the sun which was already climbing and flooding the world with pale gold light. And the sky above the hills was rosy and green. No, you couldn't get that in Glasgow. Down by the burn the cows were lowing and having their morning drink, and in the fir tree at the side of the cottage birds were chirping as if it was their last dawn. Apart from that, nothing else was moving.

I dressed, made tea and took a mugful to drink on the

front step. It was great sitting there all by myself drinking hot tea and enjoying the freshness of the air. My family wouldn't have believed it if they could have seen me. I'm not noted for my early rising. My mother usually calls me at twenty-past eight for the last time. "I'm not calling you again, Maggie McKinley," she informs me. "You can just be late for school. It's nothing to me. I don't know why you can't go to your bed at a decent hour." I was going to bed at a decent hour here, nobody could deny that. In Glasgow my light burns till midnight, and sometimes after. I read till my eyes are ready to fall out.

When I'd finished my tea I sluiced my face under the tap in the garden. The water was so cold it stung and made me gasp for air like a fish. With drops running off my chin I ran inside and groped for a towel, found one, a coarse cotton affair, hanging on a hook at the side of the range, and dabbed myself dry with the cleanest parts. Granny didn't seem to notice dirt now as she once had, her eyes were failing, but she took pride in never having had to wear glasses and I knew she never would. And of course washing without running hot water was no joke. I remembered, when I was small, the smell of the washing as she boiled it up in a big zinc bath on top of the stove. It steamed all day filling the room with hot moist fumes. Now, when I pass a laundry in Glasgow and get a whiff of the vapours, Granny's room comes back to me.

She was still sleeping. From the foot of the stairs I heard her snore. I left the house, shutting the door quietly.

The Frasers' curtains hadn't moved. I stopped by the dry stone dyke to look at their garden. It was wild, but cared for at the same time, an interesting jumble of sweet smelling herbs and shrubs. I leant over the wall, the stones nearly cutting my stomach in half, and picked a small pink flower. I didn't know what it was called but they probably would; they seemed to know everything like that and carried books in their rucksacks in case they came across anything they didn't know. The flower had no smell but it was pretty, so delicately and beautifully made. I tucked it into a buttonhole of my shirt and left the sleeping Frasers behind me.

Round the bend the farm came into sight. Smoke puffed from the chimneys. The farmer was crossing the yard, carrying a bucket in each hand, his head down. He didn't see me.

I abandoned the road for the rough scrubby field on my left. There were some tricky bits to negotiate, marshy, and whin-covered, before I reached the burn. The cows had gathered near a humped-back bridge; some were drinking, others just standing on the bank swishing their tails, chewing the cud and enjoying the morning. A small Highland cow looked at me with big soft eyes through spikes of sandy hair, but none of the rest paid any attention to my arrival.

In a second my sandals were off and I had the cool wet grass under my feet. I sat on a big stone at the edge of the burn and let the tips of my toes brush the water. It was so clear you could see every little stone and plant on the bed. Further up it came brown from the peat, and I liked it then too, when it was toffee-coloured almost, and frothed with white where it broke on the stones.

I lowered my feet in as far as the ankles and nearly shot off the stone.

"Is it cold then?" asked a voice behind me, startling me some more.

I looked round and saw James Fraser standing a few yards away. For a moment I thought I had slipped back into my dream again for the expression on his face was the same as when he had walked along the road in leather jerkin and knee breeches. Not smiling exactly, but as if he would any minute.

"It's freezing," I said, and he laughed and came down to the edge of the burn beside me. He sat himself astride another stone and faced into the morning sun.

"Terrific," he murmured.

I tried to rub some life back into my feet. Pinky-purplish, lying on the grey stone, they looked like dead fish on a slab. He was looking at them too. I wouldn't have minded if they had been smooth and brown but they didn't look very elegant the colour they were. I put them out of sight, underneath me, which wasn't all that comfortable, but I wasn't bothering too much about comfort just then. I had an image in my mind of appearing casual and relaxed, like those honey-coloured females do reclining on rocks on the pages of glossy magazines; whereas, there I was, lop-sided, my ankles killing me because of the stone digging into them, my jeans twisted and crumpled, and in the buttonhole of my shirt dangled a flower stolen from his garden. Guilty, your Honour! I'm sure he could see it in my face.

"What a marvellous morning," he said.

I agreed.

"I like being out early, do you?"

I nodded. Where had my highly commended gift of the gab gone? Give a two minute talk on air pollution, North Sea Oil, or the life style of the hedgehog. My English teacher says I have my own, not exactly pure style, but at least I can articulate and improvise. In other words, I'm never stuck for words. He should have seen me there, unable to deliver two seconds on the pleasures of early rising. I was sitting on a stone grunting like a loon. James made a few more remarks about the burn and the cows, my throat grew drier and drier, and when my voice did get out it sounded really broad Glaswegian. James was so well-spoken, at least that's the way my granny described it. She admired the way he and Catriona talked, but I said one way of talking was as good as another.

"What are you doing, Maggie?" asked James. "Are you still at school?"

I told him I'd been doing my O-levels that year. The funny thing was that that got us going. We began to talk after that, really talk, to and fro, asking and answering, and chipping in, and I forgot about my voice and his, and even my feet, and let them slide from under me and hang down on either side of the stone. He was taking A-levels next year and wanted to do medicine.

"What about you?"

I hesitated. "I fancy anthropology," I said. He didn't laugh or look surprised. You should have heard Isobel when I told her. "You're aff yer heid, Maggie," she said. (She puts the accent on of course. We often talk to each other that way; it amuses us.) My father is suspicious of the idea and wants me to be a teacher. That's a good job, by his way of thinking; it's safe and the holidays are good, and it sounds all right as well. I told James all this, which surprised me later when I thought of it.

"You see, my dad'd feel proud of me if I was a teacher."

"You can't let that influence you too much," said

James gravely, which made me want to laugh but I didn't.

We were both rather solemn, sitting there on the banks of the burn, with the cows mooing and the water rippling, and us discussing maths, biology and social history.

It was a relief to have a good talk. For days I'd had no one to speak to but Granny. It's not that we didn't talk, but we only said things like pass the butter and jam, and it's going to be another fine day. When she reminisced and told me tales of her childhood and the glen long ago, I liked listening, but you couldn't call it talking.

James looked at his watch. "I suppose I'd better be getting back. Breakfast'll be ready."

I slid into my sandals. He saw the flower in my shirt and bent forward to look, saying its name, which I have now forgotten, and I felt guilty again, but flowers grow everywhere, I told myself, and he could not know I had stolen it. Later, when I knew him better, he told me that he had seen me lean across the wall and take it, and he had come out and followed me.

We walked back to the road taking a detour to avoid the marsh, and on the way passed a derelict cottage. A tree grew out where the roof should have been.

"My Gran was born there," I said.

"Was she? Well! I didn't know."

We went up closer and peered inside. Rosebay willow-herb covered the floor from wall to wall.

"She lived there with her mum and dad and brothers and sisters. All the brothers and sisters got married and moved away and then her mum died and her father was left alone. And when he died there was nobody left to live in the cottage. Nobody wanted it."

"So the roof fell in and the weeds came," said James. "Sad."

It was sad; it was the first time I felt it. I'd always tended to avoid the cottage and think about it as little as possible. But now it made me think of Margaret Ross and her sister Agnes. I curled up on the window ledge, hugging my knees to my chin, and told James Fraser the story of the two sisters. As I told it I felt proud of them and got quite carried away by the injustice of their suffering.

James sat on the ground and listened.

"It's quite a story," he said. "You tell it well, Maggie."

"The men ran away."

James laughed. "The women must have been the stronger sex."

"I wonder why. They ran, I mean." It puzzled me.

"I don't know," said James, more serious now. He wouldn't run, I knew that without him telling me. He was dependable.

We got up and walked on. The sun had ridden up clear of the hills and the sky was bright blue with puffs of white. It was going to be another long sunny day. I supposed the Frasers would be going up on the hills again. What would I do? Lie under the fir tree and read, as I'd done yesterday, and the day before? I hadn't really read much. Try concentrating on a hot day with bees buzzing round, all sorts of things jumping in the undergrowth, and the smells getting heavier and heavier as the day wears on! I lay there in a stupor until tea-time. You couldn't call them action-packed days. But when I lifted up my eyes to the hills—I like those words—they didn't tempt me either, not the thought of getting up there, that is. It might be all right when you're up with the world spread at your feet, but the getting up would be a bit much on a hot day.

James stopped to pick another flower, a feathery yellow one. Lady's Bedstraw: I remember that name for he said it and handed the flower to me with a little bow. The name appealed to me. I tucked the flower in beside the pink one and smiled at James.

Catriona met us on the bend of the road. She was in a foul mood though she tried not to show it, for the first minute. "Where have you been?" she snapped at James. She looked over at me, her eyes spitting fire, then back at him. "We've been waiting for you for ages. Breakfast's ready."

"You didn't have to wait for me." James was good at playing it cool, no matter what the scene. If my brother or sister had come out gunning for me like that I'd have let them have it, straight back.

"Mother sent me out to look for you. She's made scrambled eggs and now they've gone as hard as anything."

"Another time you'd better eat the eggs and let me starve," said James, continuing to stand there, in no great hurry to move.

"You'd better go," I said. I touched the flower in my shirt.

"Be seeing you," he said.

Catriona said nothing to me but as they moved away I heard her say to him, "What on earth have you been doing?"

"Sitting by the burn," he answered, and she let out a noise, like a snort.

Granny was sitting by the window having her breakfast of tea, bread and honey.

"I see you're making friends with the young Frasers."
She nodded her head with approval.

I was restless. I decided to clean the house before the
day grew too hot. It would be a good way to use up my
energy. I boiled kettles of water, washed down the walls
and scrubbed the kitchen floor. It was black and greasy,
and every time I wrung out the cloth my stomach heaved.

"It was needing a wash," said Granny, supervising
operations from her chair at the window. It was too hot
for her outside. She wished it would rain, and let the air
out, as she put it.

"It rains often enough," I said, as I took the last
bucket of filthy water to throw on the nettles outside. It
was a wonder they didn't drop dead on the spot with that
muck dumped on top of them.

The Frasers' car was standing at their door, and I
could hear them calling to one another inside the house.

"Is that the Frasers' car out?" asked Granny, who
could see well enough that it was. "They'll be going to
the town likely."

The town was a street of shops and houses about six
miles away; there was a church, a primary school and
two hotels, and that was it.

"They've got their shopping bags with them. Away
over and ask them to bring a piece of meat back for us,
Maggie." I looked at Granny with horror. "They're
very good that way, they'll aye get messages for me." She
got up and went to the sideboard.

"We don't need meat, Gran. It's too hot."

"Dinne talk daft." She was raking for her purse in the
sideboard drawer. "A growing lassie like you needs a bit

36

of fresh meat."

"I don't feel like it."

"I fancy some myself." She found the purse and was fumbling now with the contents. She held out a fifty pence piece. "Go on then, lass, away and ask them."

"I don't want to ask favours of them."

"But they don't mind, I tell you. Away ye go now!" She sounded suddenly fierce, as if she remembered how she used to speak to her children.

"No!" I could be fierce too, even to my granny. I faced her. "I'm sorry, Gran, but I'm not asking them."

"My, but you're the stubborn one when it comes up your back!"

A knock on the front door stopped us. I went quickly to answer it. James stood there. From the look on his face, I think it was the second time he'd knocked, and that he'd overheard us quarrelling. Granny came up behind me.

"Oh, it's you, Jamie!" Jamie! It must be great when you're eighty-three and past caring what people think! But at sixteen I wasn't crazy at hearing my granny call James Fraser Jamie. He took it well enough, needless to say.

"Good morning, Mrs McKinley. Lovely morning."

"Very fine. Come away in then, lad. Don't be standing there on the step." For a moment I didn't think I'd heard correctly, but then I saw him step forward and follow her into the kitchen with its stained and sagging armchairs, old black range, and cracked, bulging ceiling. I went in after them, past caring too now, philosophical almost, you might say. I might have known that my granny would let me down at such a crucial moment. Yes, crucial. James had crossed the road to call on me. I wanted to make a good impression on him, but how could you impress anyone when he's sitting on a chair with busted springs listening to a blow-by-blow account from my granny on how I'd washed the kitchen floor and that it had taken seven buckets of water to get it clean?

"You might not think it," said Granny, "but she can be quite good in the house when she's got a mind to be."

Chapter IV

"We're going to town to do some shopping," said James, "and we wondered if you'd like to come with us, Maggie?"

Granny jumped in before I could. "Now there you are!" she said to me triumphantly. She turned back to James. "I'd just been saying to her this very minute that she was to run over and ask you to buy us some meat but she didn't like. I told her you wouldn't mind."

"Of course not," said James.

My face was scarlet, or as near to it as it's likely to get, taking into account the dun-colour it starts with. I lifted the drying-up cloth that had dropped from its hook and hung it up carefully, as if I was totally absorbed by the task. Then I straightened some pans on the shelf. I didn't look at either of them.

"That's fine then," said James. "Would you be ready to come now, Maggie?"

"Thanks all the same, James," I said coolly, "but I've got some work I must do this morning. A history project. For school." I could hear myself: I sounded like a real prig. My family would have laughed their heads off.

"Don't be daft," said Granny. "That'll wait. A history project! On a day like this!"

39

James was looking disappointed; at least that was something. He got to his feet but didn't make a move towards the door.

I felt hot and bothered, and restless again. I scratched at my bites through my dirty T-shirt, and it was only as I was scratching that I realised just how filthy it was, from my floor washing. The morning was going all wrong, after it had seemed so right down by the burn.

"Why don't you come?" said James.

"Go on!" said Granny, losing patience, and to forestall any further embarrassing lectures, I agreed. With reluctance, you understand. But I would have to change, I said. James glanced through the window at his father who was standing beside the car, and his mother and sister who were already sitting in it.

"Won't be a minute," I said and dashed up the stairs. I pulled off my clothes. Stupid mutt, McKinley! I cursed myself. I hadn't wanted to play the scene like that, sullen and sour, behaving like a kid! It was always better to be smooth and serene, and in control. I yanked a clean cotton frock over my head, almost fouling the zip in my hurry. From below rose the sound of Granny's voice as she talked to James. What would she be saying to him? I grabbed the brush and dragged it through my hair which is short and curls, no matter what I do. I would have liked it to be straight and blonde so that I could have worn it long and sleek, like Catriona Fraser. Not that I wanted to look like her. I wasn't all that alluring when I peered into Granny's cracked mirror but still, I preferred to look like myself. My face was grimy. A lick and a promise with a face cloth, and I was ready. Sometimes, at home, I go wild colouring my eyes, but here it seemed out of place. The cows wouldn't appreciate it, though James might, I thought, pausing; but no, there wasn't enough time, for that was a job I couldn't rush, the Frasers were waiting, and I had to shut Granny up before she divulged the worst of the family's secrets.

"Maggie's father's as stubborn as she is," she was saying when I rejoined them. "Budging them's like trying to move a Highland cow from the burn when it's bent on a drink."

"I'm ready," I said.

Granny accompanied us to the door. "Have a good time now," she instructed us. She came to the gate to wave us off.

Mr Fraser showed no sign of impatience, though Catriona did. She sighed as if she had been kept waiting for a week. I sat between her and James in the back of the car. Catriona sat as far away from me as she could get, as if I had the measles, or fleas. She sat right back too, and so did James, which left me perched forward on the seat in the middle. I didn't like to lean back and wedge myself between their shoulders, so I sat with one hand on the back of Mrs Fraser's seat to steady me, and my nose a few inches away from her head. Every time she turned round, I had to duck sideways.

"Sorry if you're squashed," said Mr Fraser. "It's only a little car but it gets us there!"

"It's fine," I mumbled. "Thanks very much."

"It was nice that you could come, Maggie," said Mrs Fraser, turning. I ducked. I didn't say much on the road. The Frasers talked about what they could have for dinner. Mrs said she was fed up catering and it was time Catriona took over some of the responsibility, and

Catriona said that she didn't see why *she* should have to, just because she was a girl, and why shouldn't James since he was a year older?

"James cleans the shoes and chops wood," said his mother. "And usually does the dishes."

"Catriona's right," said her father.

"Thanks, dad," said James. "Anyway, why shouldn't you? Just because you're a man?"

"I can cook when I feel like it. In my student days I was renowned for my spaghetti."

"Isn't that nice then?" said his wife. "You can make us spaghetti tonight. And perhaps Maggie would like to come to supper to sample it?"

Mr Fraser backed up the invitation and really, I didn't see how I could say no to him, not without being rude, so I accepted. I couldn't see my father agreeing to cook the dinner. He'd no more be seen at the cooker than he would in a launderette, or going shopping for that matter.

The road twisted and turned, fringed with high fir trees, and running for part of the way along the shore of a small loch. This stretch of country was gentler. It was a relief to be away from the gauntness of the glen for a while. The scent of the pines came in to us through the open windows.

Even with the windows down it was hot in the car, especially for me, the sandwiched one, and I was glad when we had the town in sight. The main street was busy, tourists ambled everywhere, half-strangled by cameras slung round their necks, gawking at tartan through the shop windows, carrying coats over their arms for it was hotter than they must have expected for a Highland summer. Mr Fraser found a parking spot and backed into it, directed by Catriona and James, who got quite sharp with him when he kept messing it up.

As we got out, Mr Fraser made a face and said to me, "I hate motor cars. And they hate me!" I began to like him then. I had thought he would have been so terribly efficient at everything.

The Frasers knew all the shopkeepers and liked being greeted by them by name. We went to the butcher, baker, grocer, chemist, gradually getting laden down like mules. Mrs Fraser was always remembering something else and nipping into another shop. I walked on the inside of the pavement, with my eyes glued to the shop windows. They had nothing on Buchanan Street or Sauchiehall Street, two of the big shopping streets in Glasgow, but at least they were shops, full of things glittering and shining, things to contemplate even though you knew you wouldn't go in and buy. It was a change from looking at heather and nettles.

"All these tourists," complained Catriona as we dodged in and out of strolling sight-seers. I looked at her and she said, with her chin stuck forward, "We're not tourists. After all, we do own a house and live here for several weeks in the year." We passed an American couple, elderly middle-aged, Gee honey, ain't that cute, that kind of thing. Catriona made a face. I thought they looked kind of cute themselves so I turned round and smiled at them and the man gave me a little bow. "They get worse every year," said Catriona.

"They're just enjoying themselves," said Mr Fraser. "And we need tourists."

"I don't," said Catriona. She was in a foul mood.

"Dad was meaning Scotland," said James. "Us, as

a nation."

Catriona shrugged.

After we'd done the food shops, we went into the hardware. Mr Fraser's eyes lit up. He was mad about Do-It-Yourself, said James, he couldn't resist tools and gadgets. I could understand it, I'm a bit that way myself, and often come home with graters, egg slicers and tea strainers, if they're bright and shiny, that is. Usually things we don't need. "You're a real head case, Maggie McKinley," my mother tells me. "What do you have to go spending your money on junk for?"

Mr Fraser was nodding to himself, like a man who had had a vision. "James, I think we'll put up a cupboard in the bathroom."

"Do we need one?" groaned James.

"What do you mean—do we need one?" Mr Fraser was indignant. He went to consult the man in the brown overall.

I wandered round the shelves. I bought a shiny red plastic tea strainer since I was fed up with the mouthfuls of tea leaves I had to sift through at Granny's to reach the liquid, and a dish mop, one with an orange handle and orange sponge head. When Granny wasn't looking I would throw out the old grey cloth that she clung to as if it was Brussels' lace.

Catriona and her mother were examining egg slicers, or appeared to be. They were half hidden behind a stand, and arguing.

"But what *is* the point?"

"Now, Catriona, we've been through all this before."

"It's my life."

"Why can't you forget about it for just now and enjoy

44

your holiday?"

"I'm fed up."

Mrs Fraser lost her rag then. "Nothing *ever* pleases you."

Sounded like a typical mother-daughter exchange.

"I wish I'd asked Rosemary to come up for a bit," said Catriona. "At least I'd have had some company." She caught sight of me and added, in a louder voice, "And James likes her too."

We left the shop, Mr Fraser carrying a large parcel under his arm and talking enthusiastically about his cupboard. No one listened. I pretended to, just to please him.

As we came abreast of the café the door opened and a gorgeous smell of coffee blew over us.

"I think we deserve some coffee," said Mrs Fraser.

I didn't know if I deserved any but I certainly felt like some. The café was busy but I saw a free table and nabbed it quickly before a bunch of twittery women in hats could get it. One of them gave me a filthy look.

"You're quick off the mark, Maggie," said Mr Fraser.

Mrs Fraser looked a bit bothered about taking the table. I thought for a minute she was going to surrender it to the women but she sat down, since the rest of us had anyway.

There was a plate of cakes on the table oozing with fruit and cream. My mouth began to water.

"Let's forget our diets, shall we?" said Mrs Fraser. I looked at her. "I don't suppose you need to diet, Maggie, eh?"

"Not really."

I put Granny's meat under my chair, a piece of lamb that had cost more than fifty pence. She wouldn't believe

45

the price of it so I wouldn't tell her. The cost of living was a mystery to her; the world hadn't changed that much, the way she saw it from the gate post in the glen, and so she couldn't understand rising prices. Once I tried to explain, but gave up, not understanding all that well myself, to be honest. She blamed it on the new money, which she mistrusted. Things had never been the same since they'd taken away the old stuff.

Mrs Fraser held out the plate of cakes and I took a concoction of pastry, cream and apricots. It squelched in my mouth. I couldn't speak till I'd finished. Mrs Fraser was talking about a new recipe for chicken, a French one with a cream and mustard sauce, and Catriona kept referring to the ingredients by their French names, looking sideways at me to see if I was impressed. That was the kind of food Granny called 'fiddle-faddle'. She was all for plain things: oatcakes and porridge, Finnan haddock with a poached egg on top, haggis and neaps. All good stuff in its own way. Catriona was now deploring Scottish cooking so I took up the cudgels.

"You should taste my grandmother's broth," I said. "There's nothing to beat it."

"Does she still make it?" asked Mrs Fraser, who must have known fine that she did. "Amazing!" She paused. My ears were alerted for the next bit. "It's remarkable that she's able to live all alone in such an isolated place."

"She likes it," I said.

"We've thought recently that her eyes were failing her a little." Mrs Fraser's round blue ones looked into mine with concern.

"She almost scalded herself one day," said Catriona. "Before you came. She tipped a pot over on the stove and

Dad had to run and help her."

I scratched my midge bites. James moved about restlessly on his chair. His father looked unhappy. I knew they had been discussing it. Isn't it dreadful leaving that old woman . . . ?

"As a matter of fact," said Mr Fraser, "we've been wondering. . ."

"You see, dear," said his wife to me, "we don't want to interfere, we know it's none of our business and all that, but we're very fond of the old lady and we worry about her during the winter when we're not here to keep an eye on her."

"So do we," I burst out, annoyance had built up in the middle of me until it had to erupt.

"I'm sure," said Mrs Fraser softly, soothingly. I hate being spoken to soothingly: it's an insult. "And so we feel certain you must have some plans for her. It would just relieve our minds if we knew what they were."

The four Frasers were looking at me, enquiringly.

Chapter V

It would have relieved my mind as well to have known what was going to happen to Granny eventually, but I didn't. We discussed the matter every now and then at home; I sometimes delivered a two-minute talk (just like the school ones) on how we treat the old in our society, but we never reached any decision. I told my mother and father that in Italy everyone lived together, from the very oldest to the youngest, and my mother said, "Aye, well that's fine in Italy, but this is Glasgow and we've hardly enough space as it is." They didn't have much space in Naples either, I said, but she was not impressed. She turned on my father instead and demanded to know what his brothers and sisters were doing about it. They were all too far away, he said. That was all very fine for them, she said, but there was his sister Nellie in Dundee, what about her? Ah well, Nellie was a hard case, and what could you do about it? She might give you a cup of tea if you were cracking up with thirst but all the time you were trickling it over your parched throat she'd be telling you how much the milk and sugar cost, and that she was down to her last ten pence, and all the while she'd have enough pound notes stuffed under the mattress to buy and sell the lot of us. So in the end it would be up to us, the Glasgow McKinleys.

The Frasers were waiting for an answer. My hackles rose. What right had they to be sitting there, their faces full of cream cakes, questioning me about my granny? Mr must have been able to read my mind for he said, kind of gruffly, "My wife's right, it's none of our business, Maggie. You must forgive us if we seem like a bunch of interfering busybodies."

Mrs didn't like him saying that. Her smile switched off and on. "I'm sure Maggie understands," she said. "Don't you, dear?" I wasn't meant to answer that for she sailed on, "One must have concern for one's neighbours."

"Let's all have another cake." Mr offered me the plate. I had had my eye on a fat chocolate eclair but I'd lost my appetite now. Granny was a worry, there was no doubt about it. Catriona took the eclair.

"James tells me your great-great-grandmother was evicted from Greenyards," said Mr Fraser. "I expect you know the Rosses suffered greatly in the Clearances? Their glens were emptied one by one." He went on to tell me how they'd been cleared from Glencalvie, the other estate in Strathcarron nine years before Greenyards, and the people had had to take shelter in the churchyard on a cold, wet, week-end, with their young and their old. There had been twenty-three children under the age of ten years. By the end of the week all those Rosses had gone; no one knew exactly where. But they scratched their names and messages on the windows of the church. 'Glencalvie is a wilderness blow ship them to the colony . . . The Glencalvie Rosses.' Mr Fraser had seen the messages. He was very interesting when he started talking about things like that. I had a sudden inspiration. I

49

would do my history project on the clearance of the Rosses! I told Mr Fraser and he talked about it enthusiastically, promising to lend me books, give me help, etc. Catriona and her mother went back to their French recipes.

As we were leaving the café, the Frasers remembered that they hadn't sent any picture postcards yet, so we went into the newsagent's and they bought about a dozen which they proceeded to write, covering each card with small neat writing, describing the flora and fauna of the hills, or French recipes, or whatever, and I bought two, one for my family and one for my friend Isobel. To the family I said: 'Granny fine. Weather hot. Letter following.' I had left it at home. To Isobel: 'Greetings from Dragsville, Inverness-shire. The place jumps from morning till night, with midges, and other equally groovy creatures. There's a nice guy holed up across the road from Granny's, but his sister is yuck!' I looked up quickly, covering the card with my forearm. Catriona was gazing at me as if she had X-Ray eyes. I didn't care. She was probably writing something just as nasty about me to her friend Rosemary. I hadn't felt this narky to another girl for ages: return to childhood. I grinned. It must have been the heat.

We stuck on our stamps and dropped the cards into the pillar box.

"That's a good job done," said Mrs Fraser.

"I hate writing postcards," said James.

"People expect them," said his mother. "It makes them feel good to be remembered."

We got into the car which felt like an oven. I sat by the window this time and allowed James to have the middle position. The leather burnt our thighs; we were glad to move and feel a breeze.

"I'm going to lie in the sun and get a tan," said Catriona.

"I shall go to sleep," said James.

"I think I might start on my cupboard," said Mr Fraser.

Mrs Fraser did not say what she would do, but I didn't doubt that it would be something useful, like making a patchwork quilt or jam, or basket weaving, but I couldn't see her sleeping under the giant sunflowers. She made me feel lazy, that was the trouble. I knew what I was going to do: lie under the tree with a book. Anyway, that was what I thought I was going to do.

Granny was standing at the gate looking as if she hadn't moved since we'd left her there. She wanted to know what it was like in the town and when Mr Fraser told her it was seething with tourists she shook her head. It was only what she expected.

"Thanks for taking the lassie with you," she said.

"Pleasure," said Mr Fraser. "See you this evening, Maggie. Maggie's coming to supper, Mrs McKinley."

"Well, isn't that grand?" beamed Granny. "It'll do her good. She needs a bit of company other than an old woman's."

I coughed, to let Granny know I was still there, for she talked about me as if I was invisible, or three years old. But such hints, in the form of a cough, were lost on her.

We went into the kitchen. Her famous broth bubbled on the stove. It smelt good but it was too hot for soup, and after coffee and rich cake I was not hungry. Only a little, I pleaded, but she filled my plate till it was over-flowing.

"Thanks," I said, taking it from her shaking hand. "And Gran, please don't refer to me as the lassie."

"What are you then?"

"I'm sixteen."

"That's still a lassie."

Granny carried her own plate to the table spilling some on my clean linoleum, and didn't even notice. I jumped up and wiped it with a wet rag, like any house-proud housewife.

"What are you doing there?"

"Nothing."

"Come and take your soup while it's hot."

I played with my broth; she ate hers greedily, slurping it up, spilling some on her overall. Her good appetite she put down to the air. I told her all about our visit to the town. And then:

"What meat did you get?" she asked.

"Meat?"

"Aye, you went to the butcher, didn't you?"

Yes, I had. I looked about me, as if I should find the brown paper parcel lying around. But I knew I wouldn't.

"Have you left it in the car?"

I could remember quite clearly where I had left it: under my chair in the café. McKinley, there are times when you do need your head examined, your mother's right!

"Granny, I've left it in the café."

She scolded me as she had scolded her bairns, bringing home the full truth of my wickedness. Money didn't grow on trees, we hadn't had meat for a week, and I had left it on a floor in a café while I was eating cream cakes!

"I'm sorry."

"Sorry is it? You'll need to go back for it."

I saw that I would; nothing less would pacify her, nor would she forget about it for days, for although her memory was bad for some things, this would not be one of them.

"But it's six miles," I groaned, tired by the very thought of it.

"I've walked it many a time. It'll not do you a bit of harm. Young legs like yours can go six miles with no bother."

"But there *and* back. And it's so hot."

"Don't be so soft!"

What was wrong with being soft? I'd have liked to ask, but she'd probably have clipped me over the ear. I left. My legs sagged as if they were stuffed with rags. The sun was high overhead and beat down on me as though it had something against me too. There was hardly any shade to walk under. I shall get sunstroke and die, I thought; no, not die, be seriously and interestingly ill, and then she will be sorry she sent me out on such a fiery furnace of a day. But I really had no notion of getting sunstroke for illness doesn't appeal to me—it does to Isobel, she likes the odd day in bed—so after the first half-mile, when I had worked out my irritation, I began to enjoy myself. Only a little of course, for basically I would rather have been half-asleep, thinking about James Fraser sleeping under the sunflowers in his garden. I knew he slept there, in the corner over by the wall, for once, when I had peeped over, I had seen him, his hands clasped on his chest, his face shadowed by the flowers. As I walked I thought about him. He was a nice boy and I

53

liked him, but there was one thing troubling me. Was he too nice? It might seem a daft question, but he had no edge to him. Most of the boys I knew at home had an edge; we did a lot of back-talking to one another, taunting and teasing, a kind of follow-on from the scrapping we'd done as kids. None of them would ever have been polite to me! James was so good-mannered that I didn't know what to make of it. But perhaps boys didn't have to be tough or rough, or fast-talking, pretending they were Marlon Brando. James was different. That, for the moment, would have to do. It wasn't as if I was going to marry him. I giggled at the very idea, for I, Maggie McKinley, do not much fancy marriage, a string of kids and a man who needs his shirts washed. I shall have a career and a string of men, and maybe one of them will wash my shirts. That idea amused me some more, and I was laughing when the landrover drew up.

The driver, who worked for the Forestry Commission and knew Granny, asked if I would like a lift. I jumped in and was whirled the rest of the way into the town. "You always land on your feet, Maggie McKinley," my mother says to me, in a tone of voice that suggests it's a crime. But what other way is there to land?

And the meat was still there, at the café, under the chair where I had left it. I swooped down and gathered it to my bosom.

Since I was in the town anyway, I decided I might as well have another wander round the shops. I went into the chemist and tried on sunglasses. A pair with lenses as big as moons tempted me; I counted the money in my purse, and fell. I have a Saturday job in a supermarket at home: that keeps me going for pocket money.

"Are you just wearing them?" asked the girl. "Or do you want them wrapped?"

"I'll wear them."

I took another look in the mirror: they covered most of the top half of my face. They made me look mysterious, I decided.

"They really suit you," said the girl.

I loitered beside a display of eye make-up.

"We've got some new colours in," said the girl.

There was no harm in looking. She let me try a couple, and we had a bit of a laugh together behind the stand where the chemist couldn't see us. I put lemon sorbet on one eyelid and wiggled it at her. I was yellowish enough without it, wasn't I? She said I had a nice tan, which was dead kind of her. What about pink ice? she suggested. Me, in pink ice? There was no harm in trying. Don't knock it until you do! I applied pink ice to the other lid. Funnily enough, it suited me, made my skin look browner.

"It goes with your dark eyes," she said.

"I'll take it," I said.

She wrapped it up, and as she was giving me my change she looked at me and giggled. "You've got eyes two different colours. Do you want something to clean it off?"

I couldn't be bothered cleaning it off, I would cover my eyes with my moon specs.

"Jean," called the chemist, giving me a dirty look.

"Coming," she called back.

After my exertions—I had walked a mile or two, all told—I was thirsty, so I went back to the café and drank two glasses of Coca-Cola, keeping the meat on the table, in my sight. Blood was oozing through the wrapping paper by this time. I went to the newsagent's, bought the Glasgow Herald (yesterday's) and rolled it in that. The magazine rack caught my attention; I browsed around for a while, and left with a magazine tucked under my arm. I spend money when I have it. What else is it for? "You'll never have a penny piece to your name," says my mother, who keeps money in tins so that she's never short. "I'll get by," I tell her.

The meat was under my arm when I left. There was no chance I'd forget that a second time.

The road stretched ahead of me painfully empty. There was a noticeable lack of traffic. I kept glancing hopefully over my shoulder. Two cars came in the wrong direction but no one seemed to be heading for the glen. I wouldn't have been either if it weren't for my granny. Then I noticed that the sun was much lower in the sky than I'd expected. My watch said six o'clock. No wonder I was tired.

I decided to rest a while by the side of the road, in the hopes that a car would turn up before long. I unrolled the *Herald* from the meat, leant against a tree and had a good read. The paper was a little blood-stained and crumpled but quite legible, and the marks did not detract from my pleasure. I even read the births, marriages and deaths.

I was so lost in the newspaper and thoughts of Glasgow that I didn't hear the car coming. It stopped a yard or so from my toes. Looking up, I saw James Fraser at the driving wheel. He got out.

"Your grandmother asked me to come and look for you. She's been worrying about you."

56

And no doubt she had told the whole story, of the forgotten meat, and sending me back for it. Mortification knows no bounds, with a Granny like mine to help you along.

Chapter VI

James came and sat beside me on the grass. His face, throat and neck were turkey-cock red.

"You've been lying in the sun."

"Uh-uh."

"Not under the sunflowers?"

"How do you know? Have you seen me?" He grinned. "Even they weren't enough today. Why didn't you come and ask me to take you to the town for your meat?"

"Oh, it was just a short stroll! Nothing to it."

"Did you walk all the way?"

"Well, no . . . "

We laughed. It was very comfortable sitting like this by the side of the road, talking lazily. There seemed no hurry to move, or to do anything. A butterfly sailed over our heads. It was very quiet, and the sounds that there were, were small, made by animals and insects.

James looked at my newspaper. I told him I had been catching up with the latest news in Glasgow. Funnily enough, a few minutes ago, I'd been wishing I was back there; now it seemed a million miles away, and as far as I was concerned, it could stay there.

"You've got it in a right mess!"

"That's blood. From the meat."

That made us laugh again. Anything would have done. The parcel of meat rested from its adventures in the shade of a gorse bush.

"You've bought new sunglasses too."

"Like them?" I took them off and waved them in the air. James was convulsed with laughter.

"What's so funny?" Of course, my eyes . . . I'd forgotten them, in their two shades of lemon sorbet and ice pink. "It's the latest thing, my dear." I batted my eyelashes at him, like a Twenties flapper. I'd have quite fancied being a flapper, all those coy looks, a silk dress swishing round my hips with fringy ends, and a bandeau, Indian-style round my neatly-clipped head. Doing the Black Bottom and the Charleston. I confided this to James, giving him further cause for merriment.

"Oh, Maggie, you are funny! But I don't really think you're the type to be a flapper."

"What do you mean? I'm the type to be anything I choose."

"I believe you."

"Good!"

And at that moment, in the intoxicating air of a July evening in the far north, I believed it too. The world was mine!

Time, that evening, was something that meant nothing to us. We forgot it. Until my tummy began to rumble. The noise made both James and me look at it.

"I'm hungry," I said.

"There's a lovely bit of meat over there under the gorse bush, madam. Prime cut of lamb."

"No longer prime, I should think."

"Hey!" said James suddenly. "Dad's spaghetti."

59

It was then eight o'clock. We were not going to be popular with either his family or my granny. I grabbed the meat and the *Glasgow Herald*—the latter only because I'm litter-conscious—and we leapt into the car, highly amused with ourselves. We drove back in a hilarious state, which did nothing to pacify James's mother who was waiting by her gate, with her face twisted anxiously, like any mother whose child is late. I recognised my mother in her.

"Where have you been? You've been away for hours. We thought you'd had an accident . . . "

Whilst she was still in mid-tirade, I slipped off, up my own garden path, to face the same statements. But my granny, whilst repeating almost word for word what Mrs Fraser had said, was not really worked up, for at her time of life she didn't get all *that* worked up about things. She had seen it all before.

"Here's the meat at any rate."

I unwrapped it; no, the choice of word is way off, for that would suggest the paper simply slipped from the meat. Bit by bit, I tore, and scratched, the blood-brown pieces off the lamb. Poor sheep. It would have been better to have left it to graze peacefully on the hills. It was fortunate that Granny's eyes were failing; she glanced at the joint and nodded, giving approval. I have never seen such an unappetising piece of meat: the colour had deteriorated to a strange khaki shade, the outside looked coarse, and there was a definite smell. I put it to my nose and sniffed.

"What's the matter?" asked Granny.

"I was just wondering . . . It's been a hot day."

"Let me have it." The meat was passed into her

crinkled hands. She sniffed, pronounced, "Nonsense! You're imagining things. Fresh as a daisy."

I suppose daisies might smell like that, when they're rotting. But Granny would never admit the meat was 'off', throw it away and waste all that money! I rolled it in tin foil and stuck it in the range oven which was always hot. If I cooked it for hours and hours that should bake the living daylights out of it and any bacteria that were hanging around as well.

"Are you no supposed to be going over by for your supper?" Granny peered through the window. "There's Jamie down by the gate looking for you."

"*James!*"

She didn't hear, or rather, pay any attention. She went to the front step and called out, "She's just coming, Jamie." I tugged the brush through my hair, forgot about my eyes again so that I gave Catriona a good laugh when she saw me, but I was past caring.

It was the first time I had been inside the Frasers' house. The walls were all white, woven curtains hung at the windows, rugs of deep vivid colours lay on the polished wood floors. It was luxurious after Granny's, and so clean. In the sitting room, a big window, almost the full size of the wall, looked on to the hills.

"We like to sit there and watch the sunset," said Mrs Fraser, who had calmed down and was smiling again.

Mr Fraser was in the kitchen, in the middle of slinging spaghetti from a saucepan into a collander, when James took me in to say hello. Half of the spaghetti had landed in the sink, amongst some onion peelings and dirty dishes. James went quickly to his father's aid, scooping up the wandering pasta with a pair of tongs, gradually coaxing

61

it into the collander on top of the rest.

"Shut the door," said Mr Fraser, which I did.

"Mum'll never know," said James.

Mr Fraser wiped his forehead with the back of his forearm. "That's the tricky bit. Difficult stuff to handle, spaghetti."

I sympathised. I, too, have had spaghetti in the sink and picked it out when no one was looking. Not that my family goes much for that kind of thing; they regard foreign dishes with a certain suspicion, although they are fond of a Chinese meal now and then. And if I was to make *spaghetti Bolognese* for Granny she would fold her arms across her overall, shake her head with amazement, and say, "What rubbish is this then?"

Mr Fraser's spaghetti was delicious. He looked really pleased when I told him so, and his wife said, "Yes, it's not at all bad, Peter, I must hand it to you."

"Bad luck, Dad," said James. "You'll get landed more often now!"

"What about you?" said Catriona. "It's James's turn tomorrow night, isn't it, Mummy?"

"All right," said James. "I'm game. If Maggie will help me."

That was not what Catriona had in mind. She resented my intrusion into her family; I could sense it every time she looked or spoke to me. But I had decided to ignore it, and not let it put me off.

"We couldn't impose on Maggie," protested Mrs Fraser.

"I wouldn't mind," I said.

"Good!" James smiled upon me and raised his glass. We were drinking red wine, which was going to my head in the nicest possible way and making me feel warm and oozy inside.

Already my mind was ticking over possible recipes. It would need to be something unusual and exotic, that would make them groan with rapture, and shake their heads with disbelief. "Maggie, we never imagined. . . " Maggie McKinley, *cordon bleu manqué*. The trouble was that Granny had no recipe books in her house, and half of the effect would be lost if I borrowed one of the Frasers'. I wanted to create a sensation.

"We'll confer in the morning, shall we?" said James. "About our menu."

"You'd think you were going to make a banquet," said Catriona.

"Perhaps we shall," said James.

We had fresh fruit salad and cream for dessert, and then coffee and cheese, and chocolate peppermint creams. Replete, and content, we sat in front of the picture window and watched the sun setting behind the hills. I didn't know how many times I had watched it but each time I enjoyed it just as much, and it always looked different.

When the sun was gone, and the hills and sky dark, the curtains were drawn and the lamps lit.

"I'm off to bed," said Catriona. "I'm tired."

I wondered if I should go too, but Mr Fraser said they never went to bed very early and there was no need for me to go. James got up to put on a record.

"I'm worried about Catriona," said Mrs Fraser to her husband. "She's on edge most of the time. Usually she loves the glen, but she's so irritable just now."

"Well, you know why, dear."

"But she's got to accept it. We can't go over everything

ad nauseam. We've taken a decision."

"*We* have."

"Are you trying to say we're forcing her?"

"We are, aren't we?" he said gently. "I know you don't like the idea but isn't that the truth of the matter? How else would you put it?"

"I would say we were influencing her."

Terrible bad habit listening to other people's conversations. I have to plead guilty. It's a habit I'm going to kick, one of these days.

I got up and moved over to James. He had a record going, an old Stones' one. I felt my shoulders and arms begin to move with the rhythm of the music; I wanted to dance. James leant against the wall looking kind of uncertain, as if he would like to dance but didn't know how to get going. Perhaps it would seem a bit screwy the two of us dancing, and his father and mother sitting watching. Though they seemed more concerned about Catriona. The music won out.

"Shall we dance?" I said.

"O.K." said James. I realised, I didn't know why, until we started he couldn't dance very well, he moved jerkily, and not with the music. "I'm not much use at this." He gazed at me with sheepish eyes.

"It's easy," I said. "Come on, relax. I'll show you. Loosen up . . . looser . . . let it go . . . There, that's better!"

We were getting on fine, he was beginning to slacken, let himself go with the music, when his sister returned to fetch a book.

"You dancing!" she said. "What'll it be next?"

She swept out, covering the book with her hand when

she saw me looking at it, but not before I saw from the picture on the jacket that she was reading some sloppy love story. I'm not above reading them myself, from time to time, but I'm sure Catriona wanted to present a different image. So do I, come to that. If she was around I'd be reading Jane Austen, whom I like, and not a thriller, which I can also enjoy.

"Sisters!" said James, his face even redder, his eyes dark.

"I know. Brothers too. Come on, let's have another go."

But he wouldn't. He'd gone all huffy and sullen; he was in a mood, and I had never seen him that way before. Of course I'd never seen him in his home before. If he saw me in mine he'd see me in some flaming rages; for, where he sulks, I rage. A holy terror, my mother says. But I get it all out, and it's over quickly.

We played some more records. I moved around a bit, James leant against the wall as if his shoulders were pinned to it with glue. Let him stick, I thought. Patience isn't one of my virtues. And I couldn't be bothered trying to coax him out of it.

As midnight approached I said that I thought I ought to do the Cinderella. James offered to escort me across the road, all very stiff and polite, and I said he didn't have to bother, but he did anyway.

"You never know what wild elements might be at large," he said, as we left his house. "Ghosts from the derelict cottages! Maybe your great-great-grandmother."

"I wouldn't be afraid of her!" I said. "She was O.K."

A moon, almost full, sailed overhead, lighting up the glen. The place looked lonely and eerie, and you wouldn't have been surprised if a figure in white had emerged from the tumble-down cottage along the road and begun to wail. I shivered.

James took my cold hand into his warm one. He'd come out of his mood, the moment we closed the door behind us. We crossed the narrow strip of road to Granny's house. The windows were dark; she would be sleeping.

"Sorry about that over there," mumbled James. "But Catriona annoyed me!"

"That's all right," I said, magnanimous now and full of patience. "Families are a pain in the neck at times."

He laughed, and we exchanged a few notes on our families, discussing their respective merits and defects. We talked in whispers though no one could have heard and you would have to shout down a trumpet to waken Granny.

The sitting room light went out across the road.

"I must go in," I said.

"Yes," said James. "See you in the morning?"

"Yes. Good night."

"Good night, Maggie."

I pushed open the door, found the torch in the porch and lighted myself up to bed, feeling happier than I'd done since I arrived. The glen was not such a bad old place after all. I daresay Margaret Ross was glad to reach it after the long days on the road.

Chapter VII

The smell was the first thing that hit me in the morning when I woke. I sat straight up in bed, my nose quivering like one of those dogs that go out on the hunt to the sound of the bugle and the cry of Tally-ho. But it wasn't a fox I was sniffing. It was burnt roast lamb.

I dashed down the stairs. The kitchen was full of bitter dark smoke that caught my throat and made my eyes stream. I flung open the front door, the only thing that would open on the ground floor. Granny called from upstairs, wanting to know what I was doing banging around like a mad thing, and I shouted back, "Nothing." I yanked open the oven door; a great swirl of black gunk poured out. Talk about pollution! Granny called out again, and I heard the floor boards creak overhead. Her eyes and ears might have been less than perfect, even her sense of smell; but she had a sixth sense that could detect trouble.

Quickly, I grabbed the nearest towel, half-closed my eyes, and went for the roasting tin. It felt hot even through the towel but I held on grimly, carrying it before me, a burnt, smoking, charred offering for the gods, or anyone who fancied it. There was certainly little chance of contracting salmonella from that joint now. I had killed the bacteria with a vengeance!

I flung it with all my might over the dyke into the high nettles, and in my enthusiasm, let the tin go with it. I leant against the wall to recover my breath.

"Are you all right?"

The shout roused me. The voice was James Fraser's; he was standing by the gate with his sister. They were both looking at me with amazement. When I looked down at myself I didn't blame them. I was still wearing my nightdress which was streaked with soot, my arms and hands were black, and later I saw, in Granny's cracked mirror, that my face was black too.

They came across the garden towards me. Catriona looked amused, but James was concerned.

"What happened?" His brow was furrowed like an old man's. "We smelt something burning."

"It was the meat." My voice came out weak and quivery. I was cold now. I rubbed the tops of my arms with my hands and made them even dirtier. I wanted to run into the bushes and howl.

Now Granny had come downstairs and even she could not miss the smoke in her kitchen. She appeared in the garden, fully-dressed, wearing her boots with the laces flapping.

"Maggie," she said sharply, "what's been going on?"

Before I could tell her, Mr and Mrs Fraser joined us.

"You'd think we were having a public meeting," I said, feeling slightly hysterical.

"Well, madam?" demanded Granny.

I told her and she humphed and muttered and shook her head. She told me if I hadn't had things as easy then I'd be more careful with what I did have. I wouldn't

have minded the lecture—I'm used to Granny's tirades—
if it hadn't been for the audience.

"Never mind," said Mr Fraser. "It could have been
worse. The house might have gone up in flames as well."

Mrs Fraser insisted that I had a bath at their house. I
was glad enough to accept for it would have been difficult
to get properly clean at Granny's where you had to heat
water in kettles and then pour it into a zinc bath. You
had to sit in the bath with your knees hunched up to your
chin, and the zinc was scratchy and had always made me
shiver when I was a child. It was years since Granny herself had climbed into it. She claimed she washed herself
in 'bits and pieces'.

The Frasers' bath was pale blue and comfortable, the
water warm and scented from the crystals Mrs Fraser had
put in for me. I lay on and on, enjoying the luxury of it
and the peace and quiet, staving off the moment when I
would have to get up and cross the road again.

Granny was kneeling on a newspaper washing the
kitchen floor, turning the soot into grey slime.

"I've never seen my place in such a stour," she said
and slapped the cloth across the linoleum, just missing
my clean ankles.

"I'm sorry, Gran. Honest I am."

"Och, it was an accident." But she did not sound convinced. She still *blamed* me.

"Let me do that for you."

Slosh! the grey cloth slapped the floor again. I escaped
to the other side of the room and perched on the arm of a
chair, with my feet off the ground. She would set her
own house to rights. She was the only one who could do
it to her liking. Girls nowadays were just a lot of silly

69

besoms.

I suddenly heard James coughing and clearing his throat at the front door. He was waiting to take me into the town to shop for our meal.

"Away ye go," said Granny.

"Are you sure?"

"You're no use here."

I hoped she would be able to get up off her knees—her arthritis was bad at times—but didn't dare say so. I might have got the wet cloth across my face for my impudence if I had. But I supposed, if she'd got down, she'd get up. If not, she'd have to wait there till I got back. Did she want anything from the town? I asked her. No, there was nothing she wanted from there. I decided I would bring her back a cold, *cooked* chicken.

Catriona and her mother and father were going for a walk (that's what James called it) over the ridge down into the next glen, so he and I were to go alone to the shops and would have a clear run of the house.

Once we were bowling along the road out of the glen, I could laugh.

"That meat was ill-fated," I said, and felt better. The day was good now and full of possibilities.

We parked the car and went to the café to drink coffee and consider our menu. I had a chocolate eclair like the one I'd coveted the day before.

"Pork chops?" said James.

"Too ordinary."

"Roast lamb?"

"Don't mention roast anything or I shall get neurotic and break out in a rash."

"We've got lots of French cookery books at home."

70

But I didn't want to use them.

"I don't suppose this dump's got a library," I said.

We went to investigate. We found that there was one, at the school, open on Fridays from two till four.

"A fat lot of use that is." I scowled at the notice. "We can hardly stand here for two days waiting for it to open." I leant against the wall, readjusted the legs of my sunglasses which were actually too large, and tried to think. James leant beside me, eyes half closed, not thinking at all, I suspected, just enjoying the sun.

"We will eat Chinese," I announced. "And I'll make it up as I go along."

"O.K." he said.

We shopped for everything we could think of that might be useful. I would make sweet and sour pork, chicken and cashew nuts, and various vegetable dishes. We bought jars and bottles of exotic looking stuff, and I spent more than a pound of my own money as well as what James had been given by his mother. He protested but I said airily, "Money's unimportant. It's there to be spent."

"But it's so extravagant," he said very seriously, and I felt that in his family extravagance was regarded as immoral.

"I like to be extravagant once in a while." Whenever I get the chance to be, in fact. I sang the first few lines of '*Hey Big Spender*' in an imitation of Shirley Bassey's voice to make him laugh and look less solemn.

"What in the name have you been buying?" asked Granny, when she watched us unloading the car. She had been waiting by the gate when we returned. She'd forgotten the morning's stramash and was back to being her usual placid self.

"We're going to cook Chinese, Gran. All sorts of lovely foreign fiddle-faddle."

She shook her head, but not properly disapproving. I think she quite liked me to do things she thought outrageous, but secretly of course, for she would never have admitted it. When she said I was an 'awfy lassie' there was more admiration than denunciation in her voice. Not that cooking Chinese food is all that outrageous, but then it depends on how you look at it, and I've told you how my granny was in her cottage in the glen knowing so little of what was going on in the world.

"Experience of the world doesn't necessarily make people happy," said James later on, in his funny solemn way. We were cutting up vegetables, the windows were open to let in the soft warm air, and we had a record playing in the sitting room behind us. I felt so happy then I could have danced the *Highland Fling*.

"Maybe not." I crunched a carrot between my teeth. "But I want to see all the things there are in the world. I couldn't bear to think of them and not see them, ever."

"Sometimes little things make you happier."

"Such as?" I was leading him on of course.

"Just doing this."

"Cutting up vegetables?" I looked at him wide-eyed.

"Well, together . . . like this."

I smiled at him. "Yes, it is nice."

He smiled at me. So simple: we were just smiling at one another. That is how it was: we were smiling and the sun was shining. The day might have started badly, but it was progressing nicely.

Chapter VIII

"What delicious smells!" said Mrs Fraser.

I thought the smells were pretty delicious myself. Everything had gone well, we had prepared the ingredients, then drowsed the hottest hours away under the sunflowers, and come back inside at the end of the afternoon to begin cooking. I had not yet put on the vegetables for I knew the Chinese only cooked them lightly. I felt terribly efficient and 'in control'. As I wanted to be, but seldom was.

"Maggie's been slaving all day," said James, and his mother's smile faded a bit when she saw how he looked at me. Her only son. I don't suppose she was all that fond of girls he fancied. But she struggled hard not to show it. Granny was right when she called her a 'good' woman.

"I didn't think you'd be such a good wee cook, Maggie," said James's mother.

I smiled at her equably. I felt slightly drunk from the sun and the sound of bees as they'd buzzed round the sunflowers looking for honey. We had enjoyed watching them cruise over our heads and settle in such a delicate way in the middle of the big yellow flowers. I couldn't remember seeing flowers so close before, not really seeing them in that way, noticing each fibre on their stems, each shade of colour on the petals.

"I like cooking," I said.

"Do you do it at school? Do you like Domestic Science?"

Mrs was back at being teacher again, asking suitable, interested questions. The word domestic makes me want to throw up. I've always steered well away from it. James's mother looked a bit put out when I said I wanted to be an anthropologist, though I couldn't see why she should.

"Maggie's clever," said James, who could not know one way or the other, but he wanted to sing my praises. And why should I have objected? "She's expected to be dux of her school," he went on, and my face reddened.

"That's nice, dear," said Mrs Fraser. "Your parents must be proud of you."

I shrugged. They were of course, but they didn't shout it out of the window so that the whole street could hear. That's not their way.

Mr Fraser and Catriona came into the kitchen. All three Frasers who had been on the hills were blistered with sun and health. Catriona's nose was peeling.

"Maggie is going to be an anthropologist," said Mrs to Mr with more feeling than I could understand. Her eyes sought his, as if she was anxious.

"Good!" He beamed upon me. "That should be interesting."

"I shall sail up the Amazon and look for lost tribes," I said, mocking myself. I've always fancied the Amazon ever since I read about Colonel Fawcett.

"And I shall come along as the expedition doctor," said James. "And cure you of snake bite and hack the leeches off your legs."

"And what about you, Catriona?" I said, turning to her on impulse. I felt too good towards the world to keep her out. "What could you do?"

"Nothing," she said bitterly, and walked out.

Her mother was fussed. She said to me, "Don't pay any attention to Catriona, she's not herself, she's going through a difficult time." And Mr Fraser said, "Calm off, Mother." Mrs Fraser's eyes were troubled. She hurried after Catriona. I wished someone would tell me what was wrong. But they didn't.

I went home to see how Granny was. I felt guilty that I had left her all day but she said she'd been fine.

"Don't worry about me, lassie. You're young. You have your life to lead." She gave me her sly look. "I see you're getting on fine with young Jamie."

I ignored that remark.

She was sitting in her favourite chair beside the stove and I thought she looked weary. Her face was drawn, and the pouches under her eyes were heavier than usual.

"Sit still, Gran, and I'll make you your tea."

She was pleased to rest her hands in her lap and watch me cut chicken sandwiches and set the table in front of her.

"I like fine having you here, lass."

"I like fine being here, Gran."

"You'll stay the summer?"

I nodded.

For a moment I thought she was going to drop off to sleep before she had her tea. Then her head jerked up.

"You're tired, aren't you?" I felt more like her Granny now.

"It's all that excitement this morning!" she said. "I'll

be having a wee nap after my tea."

"And I'll come over later on and see you," I promised, and it was a promise that I never kept. I meant to, I swear that I did, but I got caught up with the evening and the folk across the road.

It was nine o'clock before we ate. Everyone was starving, but the numerous dishes I was concocting took longer than I expected. My face was hot as I sweated away in the kitchen stirring and sieving and tasting. Some of the tastes were a bit odd; on each one I consulted James, and then we tossed in a bit more of this or that.

"They're drinking sherry," he said. "By the time we get the food to them they won't know the difference."

He toiled beside me like a scullery maid. Terribly useful having a scullery maid, to clear away the rubbish, wash up the dirty pots and spoons, and pass the salt, pepper and Chop Suey sauce. He was very good with pots and pans and dishes, so different from my brother Sandy who drops a plate every time he dries the dishes. When my mother goes out I make him dry. He stands there scowling, holding the drying-up cloth in his hands as if it would bite him, and if the door bell rings he drops it like a hot potato, in case it might be one of his pals. He hates to be thought a cissy. Times are changing, Sandy McKinley, I tell him, but boys never believe their sisters. My mother doesn't encourage him too much. She still has a lot of this thing about men's work and women's work and she makes me mad. We often have arguments about it.

I told James that we did. He said that he didn't see why a man shouldn't help. It was very cosy, you see, the two of us cooking supper. Perhaps that's why it took so

76

long.

"How are you two getting along?" asked Mrs Fraser, putting her head round the kitchen door. "Want any help?"

"We're ready!" I said.

We carried all our dishes to the table, which we had set earlier and decorated with flowers.

"My goodness!" said Mr Fraser. "What a feast you've prepared!"

"How on earth did you manage with the money I gave you?" asked Mrs Fraser. She couldn't help asking, it was just in her nature; she couldn't sit down and enjoy it and not wonder how much everything cost. My mother's the same, but she wouldn't mind if I spent my own money to feed the family, whereas I thought Mrs Fraser would.

"Well," began James, his face reddening. He was no good at covering up; he was one of those boys like that old guy George Washington who was supposed never to have told a lie.

"We shopped very carefully," I said. "Would you like fried or boiled rice, Mrs Fraser? Or both?"

I felt very much at ease there now, after spending the day with James and having prepared a meal in their kitchen. I offered the various dishes around like some posh hostess in the West End of Glasgow—why is the west end always the posh side?—and I could hear my own voice floating above the table as if it didn't belong to me, sounding too clear and English to be true. In the middle of a mouthful of chicken and almonds I almost choked thinking about it, and wanted to laugh.

But the food was a success, most of it, and the couple of

dishes that tasted slightly peculiar didn't really matter. We ate and drank until we could eat no more.

"That was very good, Maggie," said Mrs Fraser, always fair, giving praise when it was earned. It was funny the way I felt I could see inside her. I couldn't with Mr Fraser. She reminded me of a teacher I had had at primary school, and maybe that was why I found it difficult to be at ease with her. I couldn't get the two separated out in my mind.

"Excellent!" declared Mr Fraser.

"It was very nice," said Catriona, so I rewarded her with a smile.

James and I cleared the dirty dishes into the kitchen. His mother followed us in saying we were not to wash them, the cooks should have a break, but I didn't mind washing up for I liked doing things with James. "Sit down, ma," he said, easing her gently out and closing the door. He washed, I dried. As I stood beside the draining board waiting for him to begin I looked out of the window at Granny's house across the road. It was still fairly light outside, though the sun had gone and the sky was dark blue. Granny had lit her lamp: it showed as a golden blur in her window. I would go over and see her when we had finished the dishes.

But when we finished the dishes we began to play *Scrabble*, and I forgot. Catriona played too; she still looked sulky but seemed to want to stay with us.

About an hour later, before Mrs Fraser drew the curtains across the big picture window, I remember glancing across the road again and thinking that Granny must have gone to bed. Her light was out.

Chapter IX

It must have been around midnight, or soon after, when Mr Fraser said he thought he'd go for a stroll.

"Could do with a breath of fresh air. Anyone else coming?"

We were all too lazy. James was lying flat out on the floor with his arms behind his head, I was curled up in a big soft chair with my feet tucked under me. Mrs Fraser yawned and said she was off to bed. She had plans for another hill walk next day and thought they should make an early start. They never let up, I will say that for them, not a minute of their holiday was wasted. When my mother and father went to Scarborough they would spend their days on the beach sleeping in deck-chairs, with newspapers over their faces to keep off the sun, and their evenings in cocktail lounges and Bingo halls. I don't go for that either, and lying on the beach like a fly with all those other flies drives me spare. Ah well, it's as my mother says about the meat and the poison. Though of course *I* think they're all crazy.

"Why don't you come with us tomorrow, Maggie?" suggested Mr Fraser.

"Me?" I must have looked horrified, for they laughed.

"Do you good," said James.

"Oh aye," I said in my most sceptical tones. "It'd put roses in my cheeks I suppose?"

"I shall drag you out," said James.

Mr Fraser put on his jacket and went out, saying he wouldn't be long. He was back before we ever expected. We heard him before we saw him.

"Maggie, your Granny's house is on fire!"

Fire! The call is a terrible one, striking doom into your heart, even though you start running the minute you hear it. In Glasgow we've had some terrible fires, with lots of lives lost. Seven firemen died in one. Even as I was crossing the few yards of road they came into my mind, and I also saw television pictures of buildings burning and firemen hosing. So much went through my mind in those seconds. My granny's face. Her knotted hands. Her stiff knees. Her big black boots.

Fire and smoke against the dark sky. When I think of it the smell is there in my nostrils still, and the taste of the smoke at the back of my throat.

My granny's house was burning, at the kitchen end. The old wood was catching fast; the dry timber was just a gift to a flame.

For a moment we were disorganised, running and shouting to another, circling madly. *Get water! Quick, the door! The window!* Then Mr Fraser took over; he barked out commands, and we did as we were told. Mrs Fraser ran for the car to drive to the nearest telephone box, two miles away. The farm was nearer but Mr Fraser was right when he sent his wife to the kiosk for he knew the farmer and his wife might be difficult to wake, and even when woken, were suspicious by nature, especially of the unexpected, like knocks on their door in the night. They were slow movers, and this was no night for them. Catriona and I went back to the house to fetch wet towels and pails of water. Mr Fraser and James attempted to enter my granny's burning house.

The front door, which we seldom shut, was closed. I had pulled it behind me when I left her earlier. It was stuck, but as Catriona and I came back, they kicked it open. Smoke billowed out, forcing them back, coughing and spluttering.

I rushed forward. I didn't care if I was choked or burnt, as long as I got in there. But I hadn't really known anything about smoke till that night. It's suffocating and powerful, and beats you back relentlessly. I didn't get over the step before my eyes were useless and my lungs filled with the foul stuff. Arms pulled me back.

"Come back, Maggie. That won't do any good."

People die in fires, not so much from the flames, as the fumes. I remembered that as I reeled back gasping. I gulped in some fresh night air. *Break the window!* But James had already thought of that and was knocking in the glass of the kitchen window with a big stone. His father lifted another stone and together they punched the glass in. Smoke swirled out of the hole. Smoke swirled everywhere.

"We'll have to get in," said Mr Fraser. "She must be sleeping."

The window frame was squared. We had to break the wooden slats but they were old and half rotten so they gave way easily to our frantic hands. There was enough strength in my hands to tear the whole house apart. I didn't even feel the splinters jabbing into my flesh. Later, I was amazed when I saw the pieces of wood stuck deep

81

into the pads of my fingers.

James took a towel to cover his face. He jumped up on to the window ledge, balanced for a second, and then disappeared into the smoke. We saw his white-towelled head come back to the window and nod, and his father, decked out the same way, followed him in. Catriona and I stood outside, our teeth chittering, our nerves stretched like wires. I wanted to speak to her but anything I could have said would have sounded stupid. So we stood and waited. All the intervals of time were short, but living through them was like living through eternity.

The car drove up, Mrs Fraser jumped out and came running towards us. *Run, run!* The only way to move, unless you were filled with smoke and then you could only stagger.

"Fire engine's coming."

But we knew it had to come twenty miles, from the nearest big town, and we also knew that it would not arrive in time to save anything. If my granny was to be saved, it was James and his father who would do it.

"Peter," called Mrs Fraser urgently.

There was no answer, she probably hadn't expected one. I think she just wanted to say his name. They could not have heard her. The noise was tremendous, a mixture of crackling and roaring. I could hardly swallow, my throat and mouth felt so rough. Then I saw figures at the window.

"Bring another towel," gasped Mr Fraser.

We had one ready. We passed it.

"We're trying to lift her up. She was in the kitchen."

We stood as close to the window as we could without the fumes gassing us. Dimly, we saw them. The two figures were moving, dragging a heavy weight between them, coming inch by inch nearer to us. We heard their breath labouring even through the noise of the fire.

They were at the window. With a big effort, they heaved Granny upward and we caught her shoulders. She was a big woman, still heavy in spite of her age, and unconscious, she weighed a ton.

Between the five of us, the two inside, and three outside, we eased her through the jagged hole of the window. Catriona, her mother and I laid her on the grass. Her head lolled to one side, her eyes were closed. In the light of the fire, she looked ghastly.

"Is she dead?" I cried.

"Let's pull her clear," said Mrs Fraser.

Even as she spoke a cinder fell on my arm. I brushed it off impatiently. We dragged Granny over the grass. We could only drag, she was too heavy, we had no energy to lift, and there was no time to rest. We took her to the patch of ground next to the gate post.

"Run for blankets, Catriona," said Mrs Fraser.

Catriona ran, I stayed by Granny, Mrs Fraser went back to the cottage. Flames were coming out of the roof now and had spread right along to the other end of the house. I saw Mrs Fraser reach up her arms to help the men out. One figure came to the window and half-fell, half-rolled, through the window on to the grass. I knew it would be James for his father would make him leave first. For a moment nothing else happened.

What if his father didn't get out? My heart missed a beat, I felt it, and then it thudded when it started again.

Now Mr Fraser was at the window. And his clothes were on fire! I got up and ran and seized a bucket. I flung the water at him so that he reeled for an instant before he surged forward again. Mrs Fraser and James hauled him through.

We brought him down to the gate post to lie beside Granny. He was conscious and he spoke, saying he was all right. We poured more water over his clothes. Catriona came with blankets and more towels, and we camped by the gate post in the dark like dirty, wet, smoke-filled gipsies, and in front of us the cottage burned like a torch, lighting up the sky. Everything Granny had was in that house. I felt as if all the years of her life were burning away in front of my eyes. I wondered if her life was gone too. I crouched beside her with my hands on her arm, willing her to live. But she was an old woman. Could I expect her to live after all that? But I did. I did! The expectation burned in me as fiercely as the fire.

We sat and waited for the fire engines and ambulance. We did not speak.

PART II
The Aftermath

Chapter I

The day after. There are some days that I'd never want to live through again. That was one of them.

Granny's cottage was a scorched shell, soggy inside from the water poured on by the firemen's hoses, yet still smoking a little at the same time. Jaggy black rafters stood out against the bright blue sky, reminding me of driftwood I'd seen on the seashore. The roof had fallen in. Inside was chaotic: blackened, broken, destroyed, gutted, just like those other cottages along the glen. A clearance had taken place.

Two fire engines had come in the night, and an ambulance. The ambulance took Granny and Mr Fraser, and I went with them, leaving Mrs Fraser, James and Catriona to watch over the putting out of the fire. It had taken hours, they said; every inch of the cottage had been alight. The fire had lit up the glen for miles and by daylight a number of sightseers had collected.

Granny was whipped away on the stretcher as soon as we reached the cottage hospital in the town. Mr Fraser also disappeared, led off by a nurse in a crackling white uniform, to have his burns attended to. I sat in the corridor on a hard chair feeling so tired that it was all I could do to stay upright. I thought about my Granny and wished someone would come and tell me if she was alive or dead.

If she was dead, it would be my fault.

If I had gone across earlier I might have saved the house from burning.

If I hadn't burnt the lamb in the first place then Granny wouldn't have been so tired that she knocked over the lamp, for she must have knocked over the lamp and started the fire, I felt convinced of that.

If I had thought of her more than about enjoying myself then none of this would have happened.

Maggie McKinley, you are guilty!

A nurse whisked past. I called after her and she looked back and said, "Shush now, we know nothing yet. We'll let you know as soon as we do. But the gentleman is all right."

She came back a little later and took me into a side room and told me to lie down. No, there was still no news of Granny, she was unconscious, but the nurse thought I needed a rest. She said I looked worn out, and there was nothing I could do. I lay down on top of a bed, she put a blanket on top of me, and I dropped into oblivion, like a stone falling, struggling back to the surface again only when she returned some hours later with a cup of tea. Sun was streaming into the room. "Come on, drink this," she said, and I did, like a good child. There was no change yet in Granny's condition but Mr Fraser was well enough to return home and his wife had come for him. And for me too.

I protested but everyone told me to go back to the glen and news would be sent as soon as there was any.

"You're just waiting for her to die, aren't you?" I said to the doctor.

"No," he said. "We don't know yet. She's hanging on."

So Mr and Mrs Fraser and I drove back.

"You must come and stay with us of course, dear," said Mrs Fraser.

"Oh no, I couldn't do that," I said quickly, for I hate staying with people. I feel restless and can't settle. It's all right staying the odd night with Isobel but living with the Frasers—a different kettle of fish that. "I'll find an odd corner at Granny's to curl up in."

"I'm afraid you couldn't do that," said Mrs Fraser gently.

I saw why of course as soon as we turned the corner in the road and the houses came into view, theirs and Granny's.

"You can share Catriona's room," said Mrs Fraser.

My heart dropped even further, if that was possible. It was just about at the bottom already. At that moment all I wanted to do was to go home, back to Glasgow and the old familiar streets, back to Sandy and Jean, and my mother and father, and Isobel round the corner. I hated the glen again, much worse than before. It used to seem like a place of death to me; for a few sunny days I had forgotten that whilst I dallied around with James Fraser, but now the feeling was back with me. I stood in front of the Frasers' picture window and looked out at the harsh ridge of the hills and the old ruined cottages, and then turned my head and saw the charred heap where my granny had lived.

But I could not leave because of her, I must stay as long as she was in hospital. Or as long as she lived. I shivered. She *must* live. And if she lived, what would happen to her? The thought occurred to me for the first time. She had lost her home. But I put the question out of my mind for there were other things to be settled first.

"You'll have to see what your father wants to do," said Mr Fraser.

We had sent him a telegram before we left the town. My parents don't have a telephone though I'm always telling them that they should, it would come in handy; but my father says, "Oh aye, for you to blether on!"

He would not come that day, but probably the next. So I would have to spend at least one night sleeping on the bunk under Catriona. As it turned out, I slept there for more than four weeks.

I had a bath and Mrs Fraser lent me some clothes of Catriona's. The jeans were too long but I rolled them up at the bottoms and tightened the waist with a belt belonging to James.

Then I went out. Alone. I want to be alone, I told James, who couldn't seem to understand. Of course the Frasers have this great togetherness thing and they hate leaving you alone. I marched off leaving James looking bothered. I took the road towards town, went along it for about two miles, as far as the old church, which was shut up and unused now. Behind it was the graveyard where my ancestors are buried. I wasn't being morbid going in there to poke around amongst the old grave stones: I just wanted to make sure Margaret and Agnes Ross had existed. I found their graves near the back wall, almost overgrown with grass and weeds.

AGNES ROSS, OF STRATHCARRON
ROSS-SHIRE
DIED 10th APRIL 1854
AGED SEVENTEEN YEARS

And then beside the grave I found that of MAR-GARET ROSS GRANT who had died at the ripe old age of seventy-nine, and her husband JAMES GRANT who had died in the same year, aged eighty-two. I was glad they had had a good long life together. It seemed to make up for Agnes and their eviction from their home in Strathcarron. I saw too the graves of my granny's mother and father, and of my grandfather, the forester. I gathered wild flowers and laid some in front of each headstone.

Then I left them all to lie at peace in the sun. I went back along the glen, skirting the Frasers' house by sneaking along the river bank. I stopped briefly at the cottage, the one where Margaret Ross had come on a cold night with her dying sister. I thought about her, and then about the next Margaret, my granny. And then I thought of me. Three Margarets. It was like a chain. I could almost feel them standing there beside me, linking hands. You're off your head, Maggie McKinley! That's what Isobel would have said to me, my mother too likely, but no, I wasn't, and they were there all right, inside me.

I went on to the road and walked right up to the head of the glen. The burn ran close to the road now, getting narrower and narrower the higher I climbed. The trees petered out; heather, bracken and stones covered the moor. The air seemed thick and heavy; I felt it weighing down and closing in on me.

At the head of the glen I stopped and sat down. They must all have walked up here often, even my father, and sat, like I was doing, looking back down the glen. I sat there until James came chugging along the road in his father's car looking for me.

"We were worried about you," he said.

"You shouldn't have been. I can look after myself."

"But you've been away for hours." James glanced up at the sky. "It's going to rain."

I glanced upwards too. The last time that day I'd looked at the sky it had been blue above the rafters of Granny's cottage; now it was leaden grey, the colour of steel. The end of the good weather. It seemed fitting.

The first drops of rain fell. A big one splattered across my cheek.

"Come on," said James, taking my hand and hauling me up. I didn't want to move, I'd rather have liked to have got soaked and felt the rain pouring down me. Washing away my guilt! My guilt sat inside me like a big ball stuck in my throat.

The rain was turning to hail, stinging our faces, lashing our arms and legs. We ran down to the road-end where James had parked the car. We dived inside, slamming the doors, shaking water from our heads like wet dogs. Rain poured over the car in torrents. Thunder banged overhead, followed immediately by a bright flash of lightning above the top of the hill. Another bang, another flash.

"It's close," said James.

I forgot myself. The storm hypnotised me. The noise of the thunder was gigantic, the lightning startling. It was weird and fantastic, like a visitation from another world.

We sat there in the shelter of the car and watched the storm raging over the tops of the mountains. I wondered what the animals and birds would be doing with all that madness let loose around them. Sheltering too, I supposed. James and I didn't speak; we wouldn't have heard a word anyway. I don't know how long the thunder and lightning lasted, but when it gradually faded and moved farther away and the rain fell in thick straight sheets, James and I turned to one another. I was glad now not to be alone.

"Are you all right?" he asked.

I nodded.

"Try not to worry about your granny too much. I'm sure she'll be all right."

"I wish I was!" And then, horror of horrors, I began to cry, and was unable to stop tears spilling out all over me and him. But I needed that cry, it released the ball in my throat, and I was able to talk to him. "It's my fault, James. It's all my fault!"

"No, it's not." He spoke to me gently. He was really very gentle for a boy. I thought of our Sandy and couldn't imagine him comforting anybody. But how do I know, for I'm only his sister? But he gets embarrassed when anyone starts weeping or being upset. We don't go in much for crying in our family. I prefer to gnash my teeth and stamp my feet when things go wrong. But there are times when you must cry, you know it from the way you're blocked up inside, and that was one of them. "It couldn't be your fault, Maggie," James was saying. "It could have happened any time. It could have happened in the winter when nobody was about and she might have been burnt with the house."

I shuddered at the thought. He was right. And yet a niggle lingered, still does, and maybe always will. It seems to me there's always something more you could have done about somebody. But often you don't know it until it's too late.

Chapter II

Granny recovered consciousness the next morning. She must have been as tough as the old boots she used to wear. The doctor said she was amazing.

"You can go in for a few minutes," he said. "But don't tire her."

James, who had driven me into town, waited outside. I tiptoed into Granny's room.

"Is that you, Maggie?" she demanded in a surprisingly loud voice. She usually spoke loudly, since she was a little deaf, but I had expected her to be weak and produce a sound barely above a whisper.

She lay on her back in the bed, with bandages on her bent hands. Her head and face had miraculously escaped the fire; she had only a bruise and small cut on her forehead.

"How are you, Gran?" I sat on the chair beside the bed and looked at the grey eyes.

"I'm no ready for the next world yet."

"I didn't think you would be."

"I'm a stubborn old woman."

"You can say that again!" I grinned at her and she tried to smile back but I could see it hurt her.

She looked down at her hands on the coverlet. "I'm a

bit like a boxer eh?"

"Ah, you'll have those things off you in no time at all."

"And what about my house?" She tried then to lift her head but had to let it fall back again. She wasn't as strong as her voice suggested.

"Now lie back, Gran."

"My house, lass? What about my house?"

"Well . . . " She was watching my face. I'm one of the world's worst liars. "It's a wee bit damaged. But you're not to worry—"

She cut me off. "How much?"

"We're not sure yet. Till we get cleared up. You see, there was a terrible storm yesterday. The thunder and lightning were just terrific. . . " I prattled on so that she couldn't get a word in edgeways. I can drive people mad when I start to prattle.

Granny closed her eyes. The nurse came in and beckoned to me.

" 'Bye, Gran," I said. "I'll come back tomorrow."

"Aye," she said, without opening her eyes, and I thought then that she knew.

Maggie McKinley, you can keep nothing secret! I went out cursing myself and snapped at James when he tried to be consoling. He radiated concern for me as we mooched around town for the rest of the morning. We were waiting for the lunch-time train to come in from Glasgow in case my father would be on it. I don't like being treated as if I'm wrapped in cotton wool. Eventually, since I'm no good at bottling things up inside me anyway, I told James so. "You're like a mother hen." We were sitting on the parapet of the bridge looking down at the water, and he kept telling me to be careful, not to lean too far, and put his hand on my arm to hold me back. I shook it off. "I'm not three years old, you know." I was a bit nervy, I suppose, what with the fire, and Granny losing her house, and the prospect of my father arriving shortly. I didn't mean to hurt him but of course I did.

We went to the station and stood on the platform waiting for the Glasgow train, not speaking to one another. His mouth was closed up tight, his forehead hunched up under his floppy hair, and his shoulders bunched forward.

"You don't have to wait," I said, dead cool. I wished he wouldn't. He was like a shadow. I moved, he moved with me. I stood too near the edge of the platform, just to annoy him.

I didn't want James and my father to meet, I knew that. It was bugging me. It was bound to be embarrassing, if not disastrous. Something to be avoided. Coward, McKinley! No, it wasn't really cowardly, just sensible, for there was no point in them meeting. I had a wee chat to myself whilst we stood there ignoring one another.

The train came in, and my father got off. He was wearing his best clothes, a navy blue suit, red tie, and black shoes, which shone so brightly they dazzled your eyes like mirrors in the sun. He's always polishing his shoes and getting on to the rest of us for not doing ours. He doesn't hold with modern styles of dressing either, all that sloppy stuff, as he calls it, and he'd have found even Mr Fraser a bit much. Mr Fraser wore his hair quite long, and his sweaters were colours that would have made my father throw up if he'd had to wear them. He goes on non-stop at Sandy, who pays no attention, but then I think he has to go on or he wouldn't feel right.

James left off slouching, straightened himself and prepared to meet my father. "I'm very pleased to meet you," he said, giving him his hand.

My father was taken aback, not knowing who James was, and not being used to shaking hands. He grunted something to James and then looked at me suspiciously. "How's your Granny?" he asked.

"Doing quite well now. She's really amazing. . . " I began my prattling to fill up the awkward spaces.

We left the station and took the road up the hill to the hospital. I asked Dad if he'd been born there; he said no, he'd been born in the house, and then, since he'd got his oar in, he began grumbling about the bother it had been to him to come all this way at this time of year. He'd had to take time off work, he was losing pay, and next week they were off to Scarborough. Now that he'd heard Granny was recovering he was suspecting he needn't have come up at all. He went on all the way up to the hospital, puffing and panting in his hot suit on a hot day. I hoped James would understand that my father was fond of his mother, in spite of what he was saying. James was looking disapproving, as if he wanted to tell my father that his mother had nearly died so the least he could do was come up and see her without complaining. There were a few things James didn't understand that I thought I must put him straight on. His father was paid a salary, could get time off easily for family troubles and still be paid, and his job was more secure than my father's had ever been. The way you've been brought up makes a difference to how you look at things. My dad remembered the Depression, or hearing of it, and the General Strike, and he didn't own his own house, let alone a holiday cottage in a Highland glen. But I'm not wanting to go on like a political tract. I only wanted to defend my father to James. Of course I attack him myself for his attitudes, but then that's different!

And my father was looking at James as much as to say, "What do you think you're doing tagging along with us? It's none of your business!" I should have explained but wanted to wait until James was out of the way.

James followed us into the hospital. "I'll wait in the corridor for you."

"Who in the name is that?" my father asked before we were two yards away.

"Shush, Dad!"

"Don't shush me, madam!"

I felt real mad with him then. He had only been here for twenty minutes and he was driving me up the wall already. I said rather fiercely, "He and his father *rescued* Granny from her burning house. They were very brave. They risked their lives. You'll have to thank them."

Dad looked crestfallen so suddenly, like a small boy, that I wanted to tell him it was all right. I knew he would have been worrying about Granny but his way of covering up is to grumble and bark at people. He had probably been feeling guilty too that he'd let her live all alone in the cottage and done nothing about it.

His face was sort of greyish looking. He stopped outside the room to wipe his forehead with his handkerchief, then we went in.

Granny was pleased to see him, though she didn't say so of course.

"Sit down then, Andrew."

The chair creaked under his weight.

"You're no getting any thinner," she said.

"No, I suppose I'm not."

He was always tamer when he was with his mother and it amused me to see him sitting there meekly by the bed, saying, "Yes, ma, no, ma." Three bags full! He was her boy again.

She scolded him. "You haven't been to see me for a while."

"Aye, well, I've been busy."

"You can only find the time when you think I'm dying."

"No, no," he protested.

He sat with her for half an hour before the nurse evicted him. He left unwillingly, after giving his mother an awkward kiss. She looked pleased.

"I had things to talk over with her, nurse," he said, raising his voice as soon as he was in the corridor. "And I've come a long way."

"I'm sorry, Mr McKinley, but you can't overtax her."

"Ah, she's as strong as a horse."

The nurse smiled and said that he would have to come back the next day.

"Come back tomorrow?" He shook his head. "I'm in the middle of putting twelve lavatory pans in a new block of flats. I'll need to get them done before I go on my holidays next week."

But the nurse didn't care about that.

We saw James sitting further along the corridor reading a magazine.

"You'll need to get rid of him, Maggie. Oh all right, I'm grateful to him and all that, so don't start giving off, but I'm wanting to talk to you."

I explained to James that my father wanted to take me out to lunch. James understood and suggested we meet again at three, when his parents had arranged to come back for us. My father was frowning and biting his nails, and couldn't wait for James to leave us. He had a problem.

"What are we to do about your granny?" he said, as soon as we were seated in one of the hotel lounges and he had taken a long drink from the pint of beer in front of him. Note: *your* granny.

"I don't know. Take her down to Glasgow?"

"Ah, she'd never settle." He took another drink. "And she and your ma would never get on."

"But you were always saying you wanted her to come. And going on about it because she wouldn't!"

He didn't like me reminding him of that. They had wanted Granny to come as long as they knew she wouldn't. But now that she was homeless?

"She couldn't manage the stairs, Maggie. She'd have to stay in all the time. It'd kill her."

With that, I had to agree. She had been used all her life to the fresh air, standing by the gate looking at the hills, and I couldn't see her closeted in our flat with my mother narking away at her. For she would. You'll have to change your knickers, Granny. And let's have that overall off your back, it's clarty. When did you last wash your hair? My mother can't let anyone be, but we know how to deal with her, Sandy and Jean and I.

"She'll have to go into a home," said my father.

"Dad, she'd hate it!"

"What else can we do?"

We stared gloomily at the formica-topped table with its sticky rings left by wet glasses. He finished his beer and had another; I had a bag of crisps. I was starving.

"I'll buy you your dinner in a minute," said my father.

He looked miserable. "They say some of the homes are very nice these days."

"It's not the same as having a place of your own."

"But she's eighty-three, and not able."

We went into the dining room and had roast pork and apple sauce, and plum tart and custard, and he complained about the price of it.

"These places know how to charge!" He shook his head. "You could have got that for half the money in Glasgow."

"This isn't Glasgow, Dad."

"You're right there!"

We were finishing our coffee when the Frasers appeared in the dining room looking for us. Mrs Fraser waved, I half-heartedly gave her a kind of wave back.

They came across to our table, the four of them, in line, threading their way between the other tables. I introduced them to my father. He got up and stood, looking awkward.

"I believe I've got to thank you," he began, and I felt sorry for him for he couldn't say what he really wanted to strangers smoothly, as the Frasers could. Anyway, how do you thank someone who's just saved your mother from a fire? He took out his handkerchief and wiped his forehead.

"Think nothing of it, Mr McKinley," said Mr Fraser heartily, and it struck me that he was a bit embarrassed too. "We were only too glad to be on hand."

Mrs Fraser suggested we should all go into the lounge. We were clogging up the passage for the waitresses.

We sat in a semi-circle. Mrs Fraser talked about Granny, saying how wonderful she was, etc. . . . Dad shifted about in his chair. He would have liked another drink but the bar was closed.

"Have you any idea what you're going to do about your mother, Mr McKinley?" asked Mrs Fraser in her softest, friendliest voice.

"I'll be going home to talk it over with my wife," he said, as stiff as a poker.

"When do you think you'll be going back?"

"There's a train at four."

"Four! But—"

"Well, my mother seems to be getting on all right now. There's not much I can do here at the moment. And I've work to do."

The Frasers were silent, briefly, and then Mrs said, "Maggie's very welcome to stay on with us, if you'd like that, so that she can keep an eye on your mother."

He looked surprised: he'd forgotten me.

"I don't suppose Maggie wants to cut her holiday short anyway," said Mr Fraser. "It would be a pity for her to have to go home."

I didn't agree with him, but I sat there meekly, being discussed.

"That's very good of you," said my father. "If she'd be no bother."

"No bother at all," said Mrs Fraser. "We'd love to have her."

I saw from Catriona's face that she didn't agree with her mother. I didn't blame her. After all, she had to have me sleeping below her.

I took my father to the station for the four o'clock train; the Frasers waited in their car outside. He gave me instructions about going to see Granny daily, writing to let them know of her progress, and so forth.

"Didn't you want to go and have a look at the house, Dad? And the glen."

He shook his head. "I hate going back to the glen." He glanced along the platform and said with relief, "Here's the train coming."

Chapter III

James and I picked our way through splintered, charred wood, fallen girders, bits of iron and porcelain, and singed material which was soggy to the touch. I put my hand on a piece of mattress and shuddered. It felt slimy and spongy. The kitchen was the worst part; hardly anything was recognisable, except for the sturdy old range which had been put in when the house was built and was still standing. Only a sledgehammer would break up that solid chunk of iron.

We wore gloves—Mrs Fraser had told us to—and were glad of them. We scavenged amongst the ruins, hauling aside fallen girders and door lintels, and carried out the few things that were worth saving. We laid them out on the grass in front of the cottage: three pieces of china, the brown teapot, an enamel pail, a brooch with some stones set in it, the cracked mirror that had been in Granny's bedroom, and a photograph in a frame. They didn't take up much space. A few feet. Not much for a lifetime. I sat on the ground and looked at them and was glad that she wasn't here. She was still making progress, but it would take a while before she was fit enough to leave hospital. A month, the doctor thought, and he proved to be right.

What were we going to do with her when we got her

out of hospital? The question was burning a hole in my head. I awoke in the mornings with dreams of Granny returning to her blackened cottage, completely refusing to listen to reason. "It's my home. This is where I've lived. This is where I'll die!" She was as stubborn as old rope. Or else I saw her curled up under the stone wall wrapped in sacks, glaring at me.

I thought of my father scuttling back to Glasgow as fast as he could get away. It occurred to me he'd been running away: he didn't know what to do either. He had dumped the problem in my lap.

"Do you ever get annoyed with your parents?" I asked James.

"Often." He said it too easily, and I didn't really believe him. Basically, he seemed to agree with most of what they did and said; he liked how they lived and would probably do all the same things himself.

I pulled a handful of grass and twisted it round my fingers. I knew that I wasn't going to live the way my parents did, had known it for a long time. But it wouldn't worry them as much as it would worry the Frasers if their kids turned out in a different way. My father had left this glen and his father's life. He had got something better, by his way of thinking, though not by his father's, and he expected me to get something better in my turn too.

"Good, better, best," I murmured and lay back to stare at the sky.

"What?" said James.

"How do you know what is better?"

"Well, you can't really, can you? I mean, it depends on how each person sees something, doesn't it?"

There were so many things I didn't see in any way at

all, or at least, one day they looked one thing, and the next day, the opposite. Sometimes, I am appalled at how little I have picked up about life so far.

James rolled on to his stomach and smiled into my face. He had a nice smile; his eyes crinkled at the corners and his mouth widened with it. Now, perhaps I make him sound dull, but that isn't how he was at all. At least, he might have been sometimes, for we all have our off days. But I find it difficult to describe him, to tell what he was really like, for I was closer to him than any of the other Frasers. When I tried to tell Isobel later about him she screwed up her nose and said, "Sounds a real wet." But he wasn't that. Isobel likes boys who ride motor bikes and talk tough. Well he wasn't that either.

That summer he was seventeen, and he liked me. That is all I am sure of.

"I'm glad you're staying, Maggie," he said.

"I'm not sorry myself. The old place isn't that bad when you get used to it. But getting used to it is murder."

We took the things we'd rescued back to his house and cleaned them. I washed the china as carefully and lovingly as if it was that expensive stuff with gold on it. When I used to wash up in the old chipped basin I would slap the dishes around half hoping to break a few so that I could replace them with some nice modern ones. On the draining board I laid one blue and white dinner plate, a side plate and a vegetable tureen. The knob was off the lid of the tureen but it had been off for years. The teapot and pail had survived the ordeal and were only slightly blacker than they used to be. The brooch was unmarked, and the stones shone when I rubbed them up; they were Cairngorm stones, golden-yellow. The picture frame held a wedding photograph of Granny and Grandpa seated on two chairs. It was sepia brown and faded, but clear enough to see that the woman with the straight back and proud head was my granny. She wore a light coloured dress and a big Edwardian hat, and held a bunch of flowers on her knee. He had a bowler on his lap, his hair was black and carefully arranged over the top of his head, and he had a wicked-looking moustache. They looked newly married. They were stiff and solemn. You couldn't see their faces clearly but you knew by the way they held their bodies that they were solemn.

"Looked like a serious business," I said to James.

"Expect it was."

"Granny's big day!"

They had probably never looked like that again. When the marriage day was over, the good clothes would have been put away in a trunk or else returned (they might well have been borrowed), and Granny would have put on her apron and Grandad his working trousers and boots.

I took the photograph to the hospital with me and set it on her locker beside the bed.

"There you are, Granny. That'll cheer you up when you're feeling low."

She turned her head on the pillow to look at it. "Fancy you finding that! I hadn't seen it for years. Look at the hat, Maggie! My, that was a lovely piece of silk that dress . . . "

She talked about the dress and the hat. She'd never had clothes like it, before or after.

"Grandpa was handsome," I said, pointing at his flaring moustache.

"Aye, he was no a bad-looking man, God rest his

soul! I made him take that silly moustache off after we were married. I couldn't stand the tickle of it when he kissed me."

We had a good laugh at that, until Granny started coughing.

I took the Cairngorm brooch from my pocket, and laid it in front of the photograph. "I found that too."

"It's bonny." She touched it with her bandaged hand. "I got it from my granny."

"Margaret Ross?" I felt excited.

"The very one."

I lifted it up again, held it in my hands. The stones shone like gold in the sunshine. "Did she bring it from Strathcarron?"

"Aye, I believe she did."

So it had been with her on that hard painful journey from the banks of the River Carron, over hill tracks, through forests and burns, lying out under hedges on those cold April nights, until it came to rest in James Grant's glen. Perhaps it had held her red shawl together.

"She must have treasured it," I said.

"Aye, I daresay she did. She wouldn't have had much jewellery."

"It was probably handed down to her."

Granny nodded. "Likely. I wore it on my wedding day."

When I peered at the photograph I could just make out a blob on the front of the dress that must have been it.

"My, but I thought I was the bees' knees!" said Granny.

We were laughing again when the nurse came in. She had a habit of coming in at the wrong moment. She said that I excited Granny.

"Away ye go, nurse," said Granny. "That'll be the day when anyone excites me. I've lived through wars and deaths . . . " She chuntered on for a bit about her children and the glen, losing the thread from time to time, and then she stopped suddenly and looked at the nurse and me rather fiercely.

"And when am I getting home?" she demanded.

Sly old besom! She knew her home was burned, but no one had admitted it, and she was out to catch someone.

"When you're good and ready, Mrs McKinley," said the nurse firmly, patting up the pillows and smoothing down the top sheet.

"She could go into a home, I suppose," I said gloomily.

"Would you like me to go and see the county council?" asked Mrs Fraser. "I don't want to interfere, you understand, Maggie."

Catriona muttered something.

"What was that, Catriona?"

"Nothing."

I thought Catriona had muttered, "You interfere all the time," but I wasn't sure.

Her mother was waiting for an answer from me.

"Yes, all right," I said. "Thank you."

Annoyed that I had had to accept, I went into my room and wrote a long strongly-worded letter home telling them that they didn't give a fig about Granny, if she lived or died, or had to sleep in a field, and then, after I had written it, I tore it into lots of little pieces and threw them into the bin. So much for that!

My father wrote to say that he was making enquiries about old folks' homes in Glasgow. If she was to be in a home it seemed to him that it didn't much matter where it would be for she wouldn't be able to see the hills anyway, and if she was in Glasgow then her family could visit her.

"Big deal!" I muttered. Granny would rather have the hills than her family. Or would she? I asked her.

"What is this? Is it a choice you're offering me?"

"No, Gran." I did my best to sound innocent. "I was just wondering . . . which was more important?"

"I used to have both."

"Yes, but—"

"Aye, I ken, times change." She sighed, fidgeted with the edges of her bedspread. She was thinking about my question. "Well, you see, Maggie, I've lived so long on my own I'm not needing folk over much."

"So you'd take the hills?"

"I couldn't live in Glasgow, if that's what you're thinking of."

I denied that I was thinking of anything in particular, but Granny was not convinced. She went on sighing and fidgeting. I wouldn't be surprised if she had the second sight for more often than not she could see what was going on in my head. Maybe it was just as well she wasn't going to live with us! Some of the things I think about aren't all that suitable for my granny, and it would have been restricting for me to have her sitting gazing at me across the kitchen.

'Forget about the old folks' home in Glasgow,' I wrote to my Dad. 'Mrs Fraser is making enquiries at the local council here.'

I lay on my stomach on my bunk with the writing pad on the pillow. They would be getting ready to go off to Scarborough for their holiday. The house would be seething, piles of clothes lying all over the place, Mum in a tizzy, rushing from the chemist to the hairdresser, taking time to stop and let all the neighbours know where they were going, and even Dad would be smiling in the evenings. "Won't be long now, Nan."

The bunk moved. Catriona was restless overhead. I hated looking up and seeing the sag of her body over me.

"Will you be long with the light?" she asked.

"No. Just writing to my folks. Won't be a minute."

'Have a great holiday' I scribbled, my pen skidding sideways as Catriona turned over again. 'And don't worry about Gran. I'll fix something up. Love Mag.'

Maggie McKinley, the great fixer! I had one or two ideas, though in my saner moments I thought none of them were very feasible. One involved the Frasers but I didn't think they'd go for it, unless in a moment of weakness, or brainstorm. They had this house in the glen, with a view of the hills, which they only lived in for a few weeks every year. She may just have a little time left to live, Mr Fraser . . . In bed, I imagined the scene when I persuaded him, indeed convinced him, that it was the only humane thing to do. But of course, Maggie, we couldn't deny her . . . it's her right to finish her time out in this glen . . . it is her glen, not ours. . . .

"Hurry up," said Catriona irritably.

Being a guest, I could not refuse such a request. It doesn't suit me being a guest, always on the receiving end, having to be grateful, not able to suit yourself and say, "I don't feel like it," when something is suggested.

But no doubt that's my hang-up.

I put out the light and settled down in my sleeping bag. It was cosy in the bag, and once the light was out, I usually forgot Catriona and thought about nicer things. Like James. . . .

But I was not able to forget about Catriona that night. She kept moving around like a carthorse overhead, and I would have dearly liked to call out, "Lie still, for goodness sake! The bed's rocking like a cork on the high seas." Then I realised that she was crying.

Chapter IV

I found out that night what was wrong with Catriona and learned a few more things about the Fraser family too. It was funny, looking back, how I'd thought they were all of a piece somehow, but I suppose no family is really that, not when you get to know them. It was just that, seeing them all marching along the road, back from their days on the hills, they looked so solid, a proper group.

When Catriona did tell me what was eating her I couldn't see what all the fuss was about either, not to begin with.

She went on crying after I'd put the light off. I asked her if there was anything wrong and she said, "Nothing," and went on gulping. I lay underneath, not knowing whether to interfere any more or not. People can cry if they want to and others don't have to poke their noses in, but I had a feeling Catriona wanted me to notice her. I was too restless now myself to sleep; I turned over, moved my legs around and then sat up.

"Mind if I put the light on?"

She agreed in a muffled voice. When the light went on I saw that she was lying on her side with her face to the wall.

"What is it, Catriona?"

"I'm miserable."

Well, I could see that but I supposed she had to say it, in case there was going to be any doubt about it.

"I'm fed up with life," she added.

"Away ye go! At your age!" My granny might have said that, but it was me all right. Catriona was a bit beyond me. Life was too interesting to be fed up with no matter how ghastly it could be at times. I always expect things to get better, and they usually do; it's just a case of sticking it out. I said all this to Catriona and felt as if I was delivering a sermon. It's not much in my line, giving sermons, and at the end of it I felt a bit of an idiot.

"It's all right for you," she said.

"*What*?" I couldn't believe I'd heard properly.

She sat up and dried her eyes and looked at me. She was a sorry-looking sight, as anyone is after crying, with her face blotched and swollen.

"You're clever, you see, and I'm not."

"Come on, Catriona!"

"It's true."

And then I got it all. She didn't do very well at school, she was all right at art or domestic science, things to do with her hands, but when it came to academic stuff she was nowhere.

"Does it matter?" I said. "As long as you can do something. I mean to say, my sister Jean's as thick as the dyke outside—"

"But your family doesn't care."

"I wouldn't say that exactly." I was a bit annoyed at that. Catriona had a real knack of saying the wrong thing.

"But not as much as mine. You can see what they're like."

I had to admit that. She was a disappointment to them: that was what it was all about.

"I hate school!" She looked as if she did too. "I want to leave and they won't let me."

"But you're old enough to leave."

But it wasn't as simple as that apparently. I tried to understand. In my family the normal thing was to leave school as soon as you could and start working; but in hers, that was the abnormal. It was all turned the other way round.

"Mum keeps saying some people are late developers and that I must give myself a chance to find out."

I scratched my head. Perhaps there was something in that. There are always two ways of looking at things. But if Catriona was miserable. . . . And she was getting on after all. Sixteen. I got a bar of chocolate out of my drawer, broke it in two and gave her half. Some sugar was needed to pep up the system. Perhaps later I might even slip along to the kitchen and make cocoa. I was as wide awake as a sparrow at dawn. Catriona slid down from the top bunk since talking confidentially on two levels is a bit of a strain. She curled up in the chair, I squatted tailor-like on my bunk. Outside an owl hooted, very loud and clear. We talked in whispers so as not to wake James, who was on one side, and her parents, who were on the other.

"What would you do if you did leave school?" I asked.

"I want to be a hairdresser."

"A hairdresser?" I couldn't imagine her in a nylon overall, rolling up hair, combing it out, chatting away to the women. Even less could I imagine her as a junior doing all the dirty jobs, shampooing, sweeping up hair and cleaning out the basins.

"I love working with hair. I do all my friends'. I'm good at it. But Mum won't even hear of it."

I nodded. "I don't suppose she would."

"She says it's not suitable."

"It seems to be for you."

"You know what she means! It's not good enough."

We were silent for a moment.

"My uncle's a hairdresser," I said. "In London. He's got his own shop." I had a mad idea of Catriona running off to London and my uncle giving her a job. Like most of my mad ideas, it passed. I had never seen my uncle to start with. "You could leave home," I suggested. That was what I would do, even though I would hate it. I intend to go some time, but not yet. Catriona looked miserable at the very thought of it, so I said, "No, maybe not," and then I couldn't think of anything else to suggest, except cocoa. So we went to the kitchen and I made some. Then we felt hungry.

"Fancy some French toast?" I said. "Toast *à la française?*"

We giggled. I was thoroughly enjoying myself for there's something about being up in the middle of the night when everyone else is sleeping. I was whipping up eggs when Mr Fraser came in wearing a tartan dressing gown and carrying a stick. He had thought we were burglars.

Once he found out that we weren't, he didn't mind us being up. I put some butter in the frying pan. It hissed and turned golden.

"We couldn't sleep," I said, dipping the bread in the

egg and dropping it into the pan.

"Smells good," he said.

"Like some?"

"Wouldn't say no."

It tasted really good, and when we had demolished that lot I whipped up more eggs. Catriona and her father sat at the kitchen table watching me play chef.

"You're full of energy, Maggie," said Mr Fraser.

"Usually at the wrong times. My mum does her nut in the mornings when I can't get up for school."

The door opened and in came James, sniffing. "Thought I could smell something."

Mrs Fraser wasn't at all pleased when none of us could get up in the morning. She had planned a trip to a loch a hundred miles away and had wanted us up and moving at seven. None of us were moving at eight, or nine.

She had slept through our party. We had eaten reams of French toast and then sausages—they were supposed to have been for breakfast—and drunk mugfuls of cocoa

"It doesn't matter, Elizabeth," said Mr Fraser. "We can go another day."

"But why were you all so hungry?" She looked round at us all, and none of us knew. "You had a good dinner before you went to bed."

I thought it was best left to her and Mr Fraser so I disappeared into the garden. James followed.

"It was my fault," I said. "I started the French toast."

"Doesn't matter. She'll get over it. But she has to make a fuss first."

We walked down to the burn. He helped me climb a stile and kept hold of my hand. He had a nice firm dry hand and I liked the feel of it covering mine. He lifted our hands up to look at them.

"You've got tiny paws, Maggie."

"Big enough!"

He smiled. When I think of him that summer I always think of him smiling, or laughing. We must have been a pain in the neck to anyone else, laughing and smiling about nothing, or at least nothing *they* could see.

"Do you like living with us, Maggie?"

"It's not bad."

"No more? Come on, say you like it!"

He tickled me, I pulled away from him, he chased me, and in the end he caught me and I said I liked it . . . you know, that kind of fooling around where you understand all the rules without making any.

We took off our sandals and waded in the burn. The day was warm but the water coming off the hill was icy. I flicked some of it upwards at him with my foot; he retaliated, half drenching me.

"Not fair," I shouted, when I'd got my breath back. "You're bigger than me."

"Just as well, or I wouldn't stand a chance. You're so sneaky."

I chased him along the burn and we had a water fight. Then I started to laugh and couldn't stop, sat right down and really finished myself off. I felt as if I was six years old again. But, in another way, I felt years older.

Chapter V

I settled into the Frasers' household almost without noticing it. It was probably the night of the French toast and Catriona's crying that made the difference. After that I felt at home, up to a point.

Mrs made me uneasy. Always on the trot, making this, making that, with a way of looking at the rest of us idle sloths that made you feel you should jump at once and start sewing curtains or scrubbing floors. Mr was busy enough, at least I thought he was; he was for ever in the bathroom whistling and hammering, or in the shed at the bottom of the garden, but after a few days I realised that nothing much came out of his activity. At the end of the summer, the cupboard was finished, after a fashion.

Mrs took me to town and bought me some new jeans and T-shirts. When I protested she told me not to be silly. "You're like part of the family now, Maggie," she said.

She bustled around chasing people about Granny. Usually she took me with her. The McKinley family spokesman! We were a good team. When she paused to draw breath I filled in, and vice versa. Few could resist us. The wheels started to move. I really had to hand it to her: she knew how to get things done. She demanded attention and action, and got both. Once she knew what the alternatives were—there were only two, an old folks' home or a small flat—she took a decision. And then asked for my approval. I gave it. I knew Granny would hate to go into a home, share a bedroom with other women, and not to be able to cook her own broth. She'd rather die first. Yes, she would, that's just what she'd do. So now we knew what was going to happen to Granny. It was a great relief.

My mum and dad would still have been sitting around smoking fags and arguing. They're terrible when it comes to taking a decision. Like: should we let Maggie stay on at school? A girl needs an education just as much as a boy. . . . It'll pay off in the end. . . . Well, I don't know as much, they usually run off and get married and then where are you? Aye, you've a point there but—It would drive you round the bend. In the end, *I* took the decision. I'd always meant to anyway but I thought I'd let them feel they had something to do with it. I'd never intended to leave school. One day, when I was out with Mrs Fraser, we got to talking about all this. We were sitting in a hotel lounge having afternoon tea.

"But what would you have done, Maggie, if they hadn't agreed?"

"I'd have stayed on."

"But how?"

"I'd have found a way."

"Yes, I expect you would."

Ruthless McKinley, that's me!

"I wish you'd talk to Catriona."

I told Mrs Fraser that I already had and then she thought she'd found an ally. I had to disillusion her.

"I don't see why you shouldn't let her leave, Mrs Fraser. What's the matter with being a hairdresser?"

"Nothing." She was being careful, in case she would step on my toes, not knowing whether I might have a sister or an aunt who was a hairdresser. She was so bothered about all that class thing that I wanted to tell her that I didn't mind if she said something a bit off to me, I could take it. Well . . . I like to think that I could anyway.

"Well then?" I said.

"But there's not much future in it is there?"

"Could be more than in being an anthropologist." Though I didn't believe that, for I saw myself with a glorious future hiking up those rivers in South America looking for lost tribes. Who wouldn't take that over shooting jets of hair lacquer over women's heads? "She can open her own shop when she's trained."

"I'd hoped for something different for her, Maggie."

"Yes, I know, my mum and dad feel the same way. About me."

"They don't know how lucky they are!" She looked at me with dead-serious eyes. "Women need a career nowadays."

"They only need it if they want it." I'd been through this before, in the two minute talks. "Hairdressing's a career."

"Yes, yes." She sighed. "Let's have some more tea." She signalled to the waitress who was kitted out in black and white and was about seventy. There was one woman who could have been doing without a career. She should have been at home resting with her feet up. Her ankles were swelling over her shoes. The hotel was all to match, past its prime, needing a face-lift. Stags' heads gaped down at us from dun-coloured walls, and in the entrance porch we'd had to pick our way over fishing rods and wet wellingtons.

The waitress brought back the silver teapot refilled. Mrs Fraser poured the tea, and I took another dried-up sandwich, to put it out of its misery.

"My uncle's a hairdresser," I said. "In London. My dad says he's made a packet."

She turned her round blue eyes on me. "I suppose you think I'm being silly, don't you, Maggie?"

"Yes," I said. Well, she asked me, didn't she?

She sighed once more. I could see that she wasn't all that sure herself. There was a chance for Catriona yet.

Catriona was sitting by the big window gazing out at the hills when we got back.

"What are you doing sitting there, Catriona?" fussed her mother. It must have been agony for her to see people just sitting. And as for brooding! That was dead unhealthy and could never lead to anything good. "Come and help me prepare dinner, dear."

"Come for a walk," said James to me.

We walked down to the burn and sat on the stones near the humped-back bridge. There was no sign of the cows: they would be back at evening for their drink.

"I must get Catriona to do my hair," I said. "I fancy looking a bit more sleek."

"You look beautiful the way you are."

"Beautiful? Me?" I started laughing. It was a bit forced, and got choked up somewhere around my larynx.

"*I* think you're beautiful."

"The sun must have affected your eyes."

"If I say anything nice you make a joke of it."

I shrugged.

"Well, don't you?"

"It's just . . . well, you want to push everything too far, James."

"Don't you like me, Maggie?"

"Of course I do. What a silly question!" I was getting irritable. And I wasn't being nice to him, I knew that. "I wouldn't be sitting here with you if I didn't, would I?"

"I suppose not." He sighed, sounding terribly like his mother.

"There's nothing wrong with joking."

"But you do it to avoid things."

I jumped up. "Race you across the field." I went off whooping like an Indian. There are times when I feel as mad as a hatter and have to let off steam. I won the race. When I turned back to look he was still sitting there with his chin in his hands, elbows on his knees. I wasn't prepared to swear eternal love to him, which was what he was leading up to. There didn't seem any need for it. "Come on," I yelled. "Let's go and have a swim." He didn't budge so I trotted home leaving him to contemplate life, or love, or whatever it was he was contemplating.

Catriona was sitting in the bedroom reading beauty hints in a magazine. Summer beauty: twenty ways to get there.

"But, Catriona, you are beautiful," I said.

"Do you think so?" She seemed surprised.

"Yes, I do. Honest."

"But my nose is too big."

"Doesn't matter."

"I hate my nose. I hate myself, I'd like to be small and slim. Like you."

I burst out laughing then. I had always imagined she was so pleased with how she looked, and underneath she was a bundle of doubts, like me. Oh yes, like me too.

"Catriona," called her mother.

Catriona groaned. "Why can't she leave me alone for two minutes?" She went out.

I picked up the magazine. Twenty ways to get there! I took a look at myself in the mirror. My hair was standing on end from the wind, making me look like a mop head. My nose is too small and sticks up annoyingly. When I was eleven I used to go around with clothes pegs and weights on the end of it but after a bit that palled, especially since it meant breathing through my mouth all the time. My sallow skin had actually turned brown. I had acquired a tan! You might almost have said I looked healthy. Mother, you'd be proud of me! I grinned at myself, baring my teeth like a mad dog, and rolled my eyes. We used to have competitions making horrible faces at one another, Sandy and Jean and I, until my mum would scream at us that we looked like monsters in a horror film. She is partial to a horror film, is mum; it gives her a good scary evening and she can come home weak at the knees clutching my Aunt Jessie's arm. She always goes with Aunt Jessie, my dad refuses to go. "Load of old rubbish," he says.

I looked up and saw James looking at me over the top of the terylene curtain screen. I stuck out my tongue at him, just a little way.

"Come on out," he said.

I pushed down the window and leapt over the sill. He caught me and kissed the tip of my nose.

"It's a nice little nose," he said.

"But not beautiful."

"All right. But I can like it, can't I?"

Yes, I agreed, he could. We walked hand in hand along the road and into the garden. His mother, who was on her knees weeding the vegetable patch, looked up at us anxiously. She was bothered. What a time she was having, poor woman! Her daughter wanted to be a hairdresser, and her son was soft on a Glasgow keelie. You could see her thinking she must have gone wrong somewhere but couldn't think where. I'm good that way, seeing what other people are thinking, like my granny.

James and I walked down to the end of the garden to sit on the wall in the sun.

"Am I like my granny, do you think?"

"Yes. Dead stubborn, both of you!"

Ah well, that pleased me, for I could think of no one in my family I'd rather be like than her. We had a thing going between us, as they say.

Chapter VI

"Gran," I said "you must prepare yourself, I've bad news for you, I'm afraid."

The old devil, she just stared at me, she knew what I was going to tell her but she wouldn't help me out, stop me, and say, "It's all right, Maggie, I ken fine what you're going to say."

"It's your house, Gran."

"What's up with my house?"

"It got damaged in the fire."

"Badly?"

"Aye."

She sighed. Maybe she had been hoping right up to that minute that it hadn't happened, that some miracle would come about and make it all right again. I'm a bit that way myself: I don't give up hoping till the last minute.

"Will I no get back in it?"

I shook my head. "But, Gran, we've found you somewhere else to live."

She closed her eyes on me. "I'm not interested in somewhere else."

I shook her shoulder gently. "Of course you are. You want to go on living, don't you?"

"I'm not ower sure, Maggie."

"Don't talk daft! You've years in you yet. And Mrs Fraser and I have found you a nice wee house."

We had gone to see it that morning. It was a ground floor flat in a block for old age pensioners, owned by the Council, and it was in the town. If Granny was to hear the words flat and town, she would shut her eyes on me again. But the flats were on a hill with nothing but fields in front of them and they had a clear view of the hills. From her sitting room window she would see them, farther away, it's true, but she would see the whole range, smoky-blue, instead of brown and green as they were in the glen. She wouldn't have the hills in close-up any more.

"It's a nice wee house, Gran," I said. "It's on the edge of the town and you can see the hills. There's running water and electric light and a bath with a handle to hold on to so that you won't fall."

"If I got in a bath I'd never get out again."

"The Health Visitor will come once a week and help you."

Granny sniffed, not fancying that. But that was only a detail. The main thing was she was interested enough to start thinking about it. She wasn't ready for giving up on this world yet, her house was burnt, she had to live somewhere. She grumbled away for a bit, and then she said, "At least it's no Glasgow. And Maggie, fond as I am of your mother, I must say I couldn't live with her."

Now we had the house to furnish. It was a gift for Mrs Fraser who loved sales. I got hooked on them too by the time we finished. Granny had some money put by in the Post Office, my father sent up twenty pounds ('I'm skint,

Maggie, but she is my mother'), and the Frasers insisted on making a contribution, in those very words.

We travelled far and wide, to old houses, church halls, grotty shacks in the middle of nowhere. It was surprising how many people would turn up to bid for the old junk lying around. Gas cookers, lamps, wardrobes, pots and pans, china, children's books, electric fires, television sets that would probably never give a bleep let alone a picture, fishing rods, candlesticks, assorted lots. We would go early, in time to poke around thoroughly. I loved coming into the smelly old hall never knowing what you were going to find amongst the tangle and jumble. And the thrill of getting a bargain! In my excitement I got carried away one day and bid for an enormous sideboard, the kind that needs a stately home to go with it, and all because nobody was interested and I had the chance of it for ten pence. Before I knew it, the auctioneer was saying, "Going to the young lady on my right for ten pence. No advance then on ten pence? Gone!" So I was the proud possessor of a monster-sized sideboard. We stood in awe in front of it afterwards. It would have filled the whole of Granny's sitting room, if we could ever have got it in there. I opened all the drawers hoping someone might have forgotten to take out a five pound note, but only found a lot of little round holes which Mrs Fraser said were woodworm. We skipped off and left it before anyone would demand that we remove it. Giggling like conspirators, we escaped down the glen, Mrs Fraser and I, with the back of her car full of the other treasures we had bought. It was through going to the sales that Mrs Fraser and I got to be friends.

James and I painted the flat. Catriona came once or

twice to help but she must have felt the odd one out for after a bit she ceased to come at all.

We painted both rooms cream to please my granny. White would have dazzled her old eyes and colours made her uneasy, as if the devil was responsible for them. The only colours we brought into the flat, in rugs or fabrics, were brown and green, for these she could accept, the colours of nature. We worked hard so that we would finish in time. When she came out of hospital I would leave the Frasers' and come with her, to settle her in.

"I hate the thought of you going," said James, as we washed out the brushes for the last time.

"You can come and see me every day."

"It won't be the same."

That's one of the troubles with life, I find: you're just getting used to something, settling down to enjoy it, when everything shifts about and you have to get resettled. On the other hand, it's one of the things I like about it too. Not that I wanted to leave the house in the glen. I would miss James. I was used to seeing him all day, from the moment he came into our room in the morning to waken us. "Get up, you lazy lumps! The sun is shining."

"There are three days left," I said.

He put down his paint brush and kissed me and left paint on my hair.

"You must climb a hill before you go," said Mrs Fraser with that firm determination that was no easier to get past than my granny's.

"What?" I yelped, feeling like a puppy that has had its tail trodden on.

"Yes," said James.

They were all against me, no one would let me off the hook. I was to be initiated into the mystery of the mountains.

So I climbed a mountain. I insist it was a mountain even though the Frasers denied that it was and referred to it as a mere hill.

"Haven't you *ever* climbed a hill before?" asked Catriona, with some of the condescension left in her that I used to loathe so much. She still showed it from time to time, she hadn't changed towards me completely, but on the whole we were good friends now.

"Never!" I answered. "There's nothing sinful in not having climbed a hill!"

"Of course there is, Maggie," said James. "Something essential is missing from your education."

"I could bear the lack."

"We couldn't let you! What's more, you'll enjoy it." That I doubted. But, faced with it, and once having set foot on the lower slopes, I was determined to get to the top. To show the Frasers, if nothing else. We had had to trek what seemed like miles even to get to the foot of the thing; the nearer we got the further away it looked.

"Hills are deceptive," said Mr Fraser cheerfully. He and James were carrying the rucksacks full of food and drink.

I was wearing an old pair of Catriona's boots with an extra pair of James's thick socks inside them. My feet felt strangled, as if they couldn't breathe, but James said if I took off the socks I would soon have blisters on my heels. Out on the hills he seemed different, more confident, I suppose, or just plain bossy. This way, that way, don't put your feet in the swamp, follow me!

"All right!" I said, irritable, when we were not even a fraction of the way up. My heart was hammering like mad inside my jersey and anorak, sweat ran down my face, and the backs of my legs were hurting. Squinting upwards through the trees and heather to where the grey scree and rocks began, I doubted if I'd ever make it.

"You can't see the top from here," said James, mis-interpreting my look.

"I don't want to see the top," I panted. "I don't think I'll ever get there. I've decided I'm nothing but a seven stone weakling."

James laughed and paused, straddled above me, his feet on two spurs of ground a yard apart. He seemed enormous against the blue sky. I was glad of the rest.

"I've got too many clothes on."

"You'll be all right later. It'll be cool up top."

"These boots are too large."

I couldn't think of any more excuses. Catriona and her mother and father were plodding on upwards as if it was the easiest thing in the world to walk up nearly three thousand feet. And I had thought I was good because I could run up all sixty-three steps to our flat! My father pants and puffs his way up them. I wondered if he had ever climbed this mountain when he was a boy. He was always saying, "When I was a boy, we were never in the house, we were out in all weathers, we weren't molly-coddled like you lot, we had to fend for ourselves."

James said, "O.K.?"

I said, "No, but we'd better get it over with."

We laboured on, or rather, I laboured on, and he, with his long legs travelled smoothly over heather and bracken and lumps of rock. He was enjoying himself, I could see that he was, his body had changed gear and was working as if it was newly greased. But I couldn't find anything to enjoy for I had hardly any breath, a pain in my ribs, and all the other things I've already mentioned. I stopped frequently, usually to enjoy the view, a good excuse! Each time I turned round, the glen was different, the scale changed, new things could be seen. The Frasers' house grew smaller, as did the black blotch on the opposite side that had been Granny's cottage. Cars moved on the road like Dinky toys.

Above the tree-line we halted again, and once we moved away from this stop I felt a new lease of life come into me. I had got my second wind. And not before time either. Now that my breath and heart were able to keep up with the situation I stopped gasping like a newly landed fish. My legs were still killing me but I could put up with that.

I would make it now, I knew for certain. It was just a case of keeping going. A cloud swirled below us, cobwebby-white. I had never been above the clouds before.

"Isn't the air fine?" said James.

"Great. I might even get to like climbing."

"This isn't climbing, twit! It's not called climbing until you need ropes and ice-axes and crampons."

They could call it what they liked, like the hill and the mountain business, but I knew what I would call it for I could *feel* it. And walking didn't express that properly.

A craggy peak stood out against the sky. I gave a shout but that wasn't it, nor was the next peak I saw, or even the next. It began to seem like an hallucination, or a trick played by some sick joker.

"There is no summit," I said.

"Wait," said James.

And then at last we came in sight of it, a heap of stones called a cairn to mark it, so that one would make no mistake about it. Seated beside the cairn were the other three Frasers. They raised a cheer for me which I could have done without.

"You made it, Maggie," said Mrs Fraser.

"Of course," I said loftily. "There was nothing to it."

I stood on the very top and looked down on the world. It was tremendous standing there, seeing the hills stretch away into blue shadows, miles and miles of them, and the glen below like a green ribbon. And I thought of my granny and my father being born down there, and it meant something to me.

"I belong there," I said to James, pointing down.

"Do you?" He didn't seem convinced. "What about Glasgow?"

But I did, for that moment at least. I didn't try to explain to him, it didn't seem important to try. He put his arm round my shoulders.

"I'd like to walk along the tops of all those hills," I said.

"We'll do that, shall we? Some time."

Now I wouldn't like you to think that I became a total convert to hill-walking, a fifth Fraser, as it were, for that would give a false picture. After that first venture upwards I became less anti the idea; I would protest at the suggestion of a climb (not a walk!), pleading blisters, pulled calf muscles, a weak stomach, but would eventually allow myself to be persuaded, or bullied. During the first third of the climb I would consider that I was mad, berate myself loudly (in my head, no breath to speak) for not having remembered the agony involved, and then after I got my second wind my antagonism would begin to fade so that by the time I arrived at the summit I would stand, queen of all I surveyed, slightly intoxicated, and make a resolution to do this more often.

Chapter VII

"Well, what do you think, Gran?" I waited anxiously for her to give her verdict. She hadn't spoken since we'd come into the flat ten minutes before. She had hobbled from bedroom to kitchen to bathroom, just looking, mouth pursed, giving away nothing, and now we were in the sitting room, which I had kept as the *pièce de résistance*. She stood by the window, her head turned towards the hills.

"It's no the same as the glen," she said slowly.

"No," I agreed.

"But I can see the hills."

I sighed with relief. "At least that's something, eh, Gran?"

"Aye, that's something. Funny how different they are, far away like that."

"Do you mind all that much?"

"I'm too old to mind, Maggie. At my age you have to be thankful for what you have."

She left the window, she was weary and needed a seat. She looked over the two armchairs and chose the big wing armchair in brown moquette. I had thought it ghastly but Mrs Fraser had said my Granny would like it. Granny settled her head against the back of the chair, laid her arms on the rests.

"No bad," she said.

"I'm glad you like it. It was a real bargain, three pounds it was, and there's not a mark on it."

"The place is no bad either. For a modern house."

I squashed my smile. "I'll make you a cup of tea."

I hadn't told her we had salvaged the teapot. I made the tea, set a tray and carried it in.

"Fancy that! There's my old teapot. Trust it to come through a fire!"

I poured. "There you are now, Gran, a nice cup of tea. And a fresh scone baked this morning."

She munched and drank, and I gave her a running commentary on the advantages of living here compared with the glen. Apart from hot water and all that, the mod cons, there were the shops selling fresh food every day, people close by to help her if she was ill and go shopping for her. The woman in the flat above was only sixty and went to the shops every day. She had said she would be be delighted to shop for Granny too.

"I don't like taking favours from strangers," said Granny.

"They won't be strangers after a week or two."

"Week or two!" she said. "The Frasers had been a summer in their house before I could say they weren't strangers."

"If you don't want to take favours then don't take them!" I had resolved before I went for her at the hospital that I was going to be sweet and nice and not let her rattle me. But there were times when Granny would have driven a saint to blow his cool, and I'm nowhere near sainthood. St Margaret! She was a goodly woman, very virtuous, helping the poor, never thinking of herself, or so that's how she's cracked up to be. Married to Malcolm Canmore. A long way back, you understand, like nine hundred years. I never took to her all that much. Mary Queen of Scots, Cleopatra and Queen Nefertiti are more in my line.

I bounced off to the kitchen reflecting on the ingratitude of the old. No matter what I did she wouldn't really appreciate me.

I was peeling potatoes for dinner when the doorbell rang. It was Mrs Clark, the lady from upstairs, come to call. I took her into the sitting room, nudged Granny who had begun to snore, and introduced them. Mrs Clark had been to the hairdresser. Her blue-grey hair was back-combed into a bouffant, she wore what my mother would call a 'smart wee suit' in blue Crimplene, and thin-heeled shoes. Granny sat as if she was dazed, listening to her. Two old age pensioners having a chat! Granny wasn't going to be too taken with her neighbour, I knew she would tell me that the moment I shut the door behind Mrs Clark. Fortunately Mrs Clark looked as if she wouldn't even know that Granny couldn't be bothered with her. She chattered to us in a high twittery voice. She didn't belong to these parts—she didn't have to tell us—but her late husband had; she was from the south (Edinburgh) herself. But she had lived in the town for a long time. It was amazing what we learnt about it in twenty minutes. There was no lack of scandal apparently, though when you walked down the front street you could hardly credit anyone had a wicked thought in their head. There were even two of the pensioners who were carrying on a bit dubiously.

"They go everywhere together," said Mrs Clark, nodding her head in the same knowing way that my mother did, when she was running somebody down.

Granny gazed at the woman's face and muttered once or twice when there was a space and it seemed expected.

"Well," said Mrs Clark, getting up, "I won't keep you back. You must be busy, Margaret. It is Margaret, isn't it?"

"Maggie," said Granny. "We never call her anything else."

"All right then, Maggie," said Mrs Clark, "I'll be off but don't hesitate to call if you need me."

She trotted off. I closed the door.

"I don't think," started Granny.

"Now, Gran," I said, "I know what you're going to say but she's kind and there's times you'll be glad of her."

Now I felt as if it was I who was the aged one, and Granny the junior.

The neighbour on the ground floor called next, a man almost as old as Granny herself, who smoked a foul pipe and muttered about the world under a shaggy moustache. It was not what it used to be, etc. . . . We didn't hear three words in a row of what he said. Granny went to sleep, hands folded in her lap, and I kept getting up and down and saying, "Excuse me, Mr Farquharson, but I've something cooking." No hint would budge him. After a while he gave up talking and went on puffing and staring out of the window.

When the dinner was ready I saw the look in his eyes. He could smell food. And then I thought he probably didn't have a hot meal all that often, living alone, and so I offered him a plate of mince, potatoes and cabbage. No

138

more French food! Back to *cuisine à la Granny*. Mr Farquharson jumped at the chance to eat with us. I saw Granny looking sourly across the table at him gobbling up mince and potatoes under his moustache.

"Do you make soup, mistress?" He referred to her as mistress, the old Scottish form of address.

"Every day," she said, proudly, in spite of herself.

"I'm very fond of a drop of soup, mistress, very fond. My good wife used to make a potful every day of her life, God rest her soul."

I got rid of him in the end by telling him it was time to go. He took no offence.

"Thanks, lassie. See you tomorrow."

"Not if I see you first," I muttered as I shut the door. Granny would not be too bothered by him when I was gone; she wouldn't hear the doorbell half of the time, and when she did she wouldn't let in anyone she didn't want.

After two days I knew everyone in the block of flats and most of the shopkeepers in the town too. I asked everyone to keep an eye on my granny when the summer ended and we all went home. She would be better supervised than she had been for years. And the Health visitor was coming in twice a week. She was a plump cheery woman who bustled and managed Granny just fine.

"Now come along, Mrs McKinley, we're going to give you a nice warm bath today. You'll feel much better for it."

And Granny, grumbling, went. I couldn't get over it. But she'd been bullied in hospital, she told me, made to have a bath and change her clothes when they were still as fresh as new.

"You'd think I was five years old!"

Whilst Granny was having her bath I sat outside on the wooden bench provided for the pensioners and sunned myself. I felt terribly efficient. Everything was under control. Granny's new life had begun smoothly.

Chapter VIII

My father arrived a few days after Granny moved into her new home.

"And what's brought you all this way?" she demanded.

"I wanted to make sure you were all right. It's a nice wee house you've got, ma," he said, looking round.

"Not thanks to you!"

"Nan said to tell you you were welcome to come to us if you're not happy."

"Happy!" She humphed. "How could I be happy in a place like this? People on top of me like ants."

I felt really annoyed with her then. Ingratitude! I ground my teeth. Just when I thought everything was going nicely. I glared at her and she avoided my eye. Then I realised she was putting half of it on for my father. She wasn't going to let him get off too lightly. So I grinned at her instead, which she didn't like either, and then I went outside to enjoy the drowsy August afternoon and leave them to it. I sat on the bench and looked over at the hills and thought about the Frasers.

I hadn't had much time to think about them recently; I'd been so tied up with Granny. James came every day to see me, driving into town in his father's car, usually on his own. His family weren't together as much as they

used to be. Often James said his mother and father had
gone out on the hills and Catriona was at home alone.
She was spending a lot of time sitting in her bedroom
moping and James was fed up with her. She'd come only
once to see me. Mr Farquharson had been there talking
his head off as usual and Catriona hardly got a word in.
I was doing the washing too, his as well as Granny's, so
the kitchen was full of steam and wet clothes and Mr
Farquharson's feet which were always sticking out in the
wrong places. I hadn't meant to do his washing when he
started dropping hints, telling me what a job it was to get
his clothes washed since his good wife had died, it was a
long road to the launderette, etc. . . . In the end I'd said,
"All right, Mr Farquharson, hand it over!" I nearly col-
lapsed under the weight of it. He must have been saving
it from 1906. I had to tie up an extra clothes line. But
Catriona hadn't been amused; she'd sat and sulked, and
afterwards, I felt I should have made some time for her.

Dad stayed the night. "I'm honoured," said Granny,
sarcastically, but she was quite pleased. He brought some
beer in for himself, a bottle of stout for her and some
Coca-Cola for me, and we had a bit of a party. Granny
enjoyed her stout; she smacked her lips and became quite
merry. She told me tales about my father when he was a
boy, embarrassing ones, for him, but we all ended up
laughing and when I lay down on the two armchairs
shoved together to sleep that night I thought that was
one of the best nights I'd had with my dad for a while. He
could be good fun when he let his hair down. Not that
he'd much to let down.

"You should grow your hair," I said to him, when he
was combing it in front of the mirror in the morning,

putting each strand carefully into place. "You wouldn't be at all bad-looking then."

"You're a cheeky besom," he said.

I walked him to the station for his train.

"You'll be coming home soon, Maggie."

A week. I'd forgotten. . . . The thought didn't lift me the way it would once have done.

"Aye," I said. "Soon."

I met James on the way back from the station. He was on foot.

"Catriona's run away," he said. "She's gone back to Edinburgh."

"Well!"

"She left early this morning. She left a note saying she couldn't stand it any longer, she felt cooped up and couldn't breathe."

"I bet your mother's upset."

"She's gone after her."

That was only to be expected. You couldn't expect Mrs Fraser to go against her nature. If only she could cotton on to the idea that you do more good sometimes by doing nothing. Such pearls of wisdom I could drop for her if she'd only listen!

Poor Catriona, so miserable, and lonely too, no doubt. James and I had been selfish: we should have bothered with her more.

James shook his head. "Women!" he said in a voice that I'd heard my father use.

"You're just like my father," I said, not pleasing him too much. I laughed at the look on his face. We began to walk towards Granny's house. I thought of Catriona.

"Do you know, I think Catriona will marry young and have lots of kids."

"Kids! Her? She hasn't got the patience."

"How do you know, James Fraser?"

"Would you like to have kids, Maggie?"

"Do you think *I* would have patience?"

"I don't know. You might. What age would you like to get married at?"

"Ninety. A good age that. I reckon I should be ready to settle down then."

"No, but seriously?"

"Who wants to be serious about a thing like that?"

"But you're never serious about anything."

I laughed again, infuriating him. I didn't really feel like laughing but I didn't know what else to do, to be honest.

We passed the time of day with Mr Farquharson who must have seen us coming and nipped out of his house to catch us, then we went in to Granny. I told her about Catriona, trying to explain why she had run off like that. Granny thought Catriona would have had more sense.

"Lassies nowadays!"

"We're not made of the stuff you were made of, are we, Gran?"

"But why is she wanting to leave the school and go out working? She'll have plenty time for working. I could have told her a thing or two about that." Granny turned to James. "And how are you and your father managing on your own? With no womenfolk in the house."

"We get by," he said. "We eat beans on toast, things like that."

"Liar," I said under my breath.

"That'll no do at all," said Granny. "Maggie, you'll need to go and look after them."

So she packed me off to the glen. Men needed looking after, by her way of thinking; she thought they couldn't boil an egg if they were starving. That was how my grandfather had been. My father's not much better but he's learning, for my mother's catching on now, even if it is a bit late, that she doesn't have to wait on him hand and foot. It used to be, if Jean and I weren't at home, and mother was late back from the hairdresser's or the shops, he would sit and suffer and not even make himself a cup of tea.

"I don't need you," said Granny to me. "I can manage fine. I'll need to do it when you're gone. And to be honest, I could be doing with a bit of a rest from you, Maggie. Now keep your hair on! I'm fond of you, you ken that full well, but I wouldn't say you were a rest cure exactly. And the folk you have coming in and out at all hours of the day and night!" I'd had a couple of gipsies in the night before. They told my fortune. I was going to be rich and successful, and travel a lot (just what I expected), and marry an equally rich and successful man (that part I hadn't considered much). Granny wouldn't let them tell hers. "Get on with you," she said. "I don't want to see the future. At my age!" The gipsies called me "Lovely lady", and I, as easily buttered up as the next, thought they were great.

I gave Granny a few instructions.

"Away with you now," she said. "How do you think I managed eighty-three years without you?"

I couldn't imagine.

James and I headed for the glen. Once we were on the

road and the hills were getting closer and closer I began to skip. It was incredible, but I'd been homesick! Homesick for the glen!

The hot spell had long since passed and the air was slightly cool. James said he could smell autumn in the air.

"There's a nip," he said. "You can tell when it's about to change from one season to the next. At least, you can, with summer into autumn."

I had never thought about it before but I knew what he meant. The air did seem different: there was an extra tang in it, and the trees and flowers were on the brink of change. James jumped at the branch of a tree and brought down a leaf. He showed it to me in the palm of his hand: it was curling slightly at the edges, drying, beginning to turn from green to yellow.

So summer was passing. And by the time it was gone we would be too, back to the city and school. At the beginning, summer had seemed as if it would be endless. Now I wondered where it had gone.

"I don't want to go home," I said.

James laughed. "I thought Glasgow was the be-all and end-all."

"It is. In its own way."

We met the gipsies on the road. They were carrying bundles under their arms. They flashed their teeth at me, a bit yellow and stubby they were but still they did flash, and called me 'Lovely lady' once again.

"Read your hand, sir?" They sidled up to James.

He held out his hand. One gipsy was oldish, the other young and pretty. The young one eyed James coyly and made sure she got to hold his hand. The other told the fortune. He would be rich and successful, and—here she glanced slyly at me—he would marry a lovely lady with dark eyes and curly hair and have six children.

James was pleased. He crossed their palms with silver. They told us we were lucky people, good fortune was sure to smile on us.

"God bless you both," said the older gipsy, and then we parted.

"Six children," mused James.

"I wouldn't waste too much time worrying about that."

We turned the corner and the house came into view. I ran towards it. It was like going home.

Mr Fraser was sitting in a deck chair in the garden reading a thriller with a lurid cover. He looked guilty until he realised it was only us. He had probably promised Mrs that he would have the bathroom cupboard finished before she got back.

In the evening we walked to the 'phone box and Mr Fraser 'phoned his wife. Catriona was at home and refusing to talk to her mother. "She is being quite ridiculous," said Mrs to Mr who passed it on to us. It was such a lovely evening, the sky was glimmering with the most gorgeous colours, and the air was quiet and soft, so we found it difficult even to think about Mrs Fraser's agitation. Mr tried hard to be worried too but didn't succeed very well. His wife was staying in Edinburgh meantime, until "Catriona comes to her senses".

"Seductive, this place," he said, as we strolled back, the three of us in a row, with me in the middle holding an arm of each. "Nothing ever seems pressing."

We had two blissfully peaceful days, getting lazier and

lazier with each hour that passed. We walked a little, fairly gently, ate, talked, read, and sat in front of the window watching the sun go down. If Mrs hadn't come back we'd have got quite slovenly in the end.

She returned in the early afternoon of the third day. When we heard the car stop outside we jumped as if a gun had been fired. Mr Fraser and James began tidying up, in the quickest possible way, shoving things into cupboards and under cushions, and I attacked the teetering pile of dirty dishes in the kitchen.

Mrs Fraser had Catriona with her. Catriona was quiet and disappeared into her room, her mother was brisk.

"Help me unload the car, James, please. I've stocked up on groceries. Prices are certainly cheaper in Edinburgh. Nice to see you, Maggie. How's the cupboard going, Peter?"

He hadn't put a nail in it since she'd left. He slipped into the bathroom whilst they were unloading the car.

I finished the dishes and went after Catriona.

"Hi!"

"Hullo."

"You all right?"

She nodded. "Mum's going to let me leave school."

"Good." She smiled rather wanly so I asked, "What's the matter then?"

"It's just that I've upset her so much."

"You can't help that, Catriona."

"I could if—"

"No! You know what you want. You've got to stick to it."

"Yes, you're right, Maggie. I know you are."

"She'll get used to it."

Mrs Fraser was on edge for the rest of the day and a bit

nippy with all of us. "Is your granny all alone then, Maggie?" she said. "Shouldn't you be with her?"

"There's no need for her to go to-night," said Mr quickly.

"James can run you back in the morning," she said. "I'm sure you want to spend all the time you can with your granny."

So it was to be my last night in the glen, and my last night with the Frasers. Mrs softened again in the evening after a meal and a bottle of wine. She laid off the snapping; we played records and enjoyed ourselves. Even Catriona smiled and laughed and was persuaded to dance.

Before we went to bed James and I took a short walk along the road. It was dark: there was no moon, and the days were shortening. He put his arm round me and I snuggled against him. He felt warm.

"I wish summer could have gone on and on," he said.

Yes, so did I.

We went as far as the cottage where Granny had been born, then turned homeward, back down the glen. An owl hooted but apart from him, the night was dead quiet.

Catriona and I lay in the dark and talked for a long time. We promised to write to one another, and she said she would let me know how the hairdressing went.

I awakened early even though we had gone to sleep late. Catriona was sleeping deeply overhead and the sun was filtering between the curtains. I listened. A bird was calling outside. I got up and tiptoed in my pyjamas to the sitting room.

I drew back the curtains. Pink and green light was flooding the tops of the hills. It was beautiful. I was going

to miss that when I was back in Glasgow.
    And Catriona.
    And Mr and Mrs Fraser.
    And James.
    And my granny.

Chapter IX

My suitcase stood by the door with several bulging paper carriers beside it.

"Are you sure you have everything?" asked Granny.

I looked over at the bulging carriers and didn't have to answer. She was fidgeting around by the sideboard; I shifted from foot to foot wishing I was away, now that I was going. I hate goodbyes—don't really know how to say them. Outside in the street the Frasers waited in their car. They were taking me home to Glasgow.

"Maggie—" Granny turned round and held out her hand. In it lay the Cairngorm brooch. "I want you to have this."

"Oh Granny!" I whooped with delight, nearly strangling her when I put my arms round her neck. "Do you mean it? Really?"

"Course I mean it." She sounded a bit thick in the throat. "Away with you now. Take it!" She thrust it into my hand and turned back to the sideboard. She held the edge of it between her fingers as if she needed support.

"Are you all right, Gran?"

Of course she was all right, she would never admit to being anything else. She began to scold me. The Frasers were waiting for me and it was time I stopped dithering.

I pinned the brooch on to my shirt. It probably looked daft on blue denim but I didn't care.

"See you next summer, Gran."

She nodded. "You'll come for your holidays?"

"The whole summer." Just like this one. But could there ever be another like it? "I might come at Easter too. Yes, I will!"

I kissed her creased cheek, she clutched my hand for a moment in her knotted one, and then she let me go, giving me a little push.

"Tell that father of yours I'm wanting to see him before next year!"

"Right!"

I picked up my case and bags. Granny shook her head and said I looked like a tinker with all those bundles. I staggered down the path dropping bits and pieces, and James jumped out of the car to help. Mr Farquharson and Mrs Clark were out to wave me off, as well as some of the other tenants. Mr Fraser just managed to get all my things into the car. I sat sandwiched between James and Catriona clutching two of the carrier bags on my knee.

Mr Fraser started the car, tooted the horn, everybody waved. Granny was standing by her window. She didn't wave, she just stood there until we were out of sight.

"She'll be all right now, Maggie," said Mrs Fraser. "There's no need to worry about her."

"No," I said meekly. I'd discovered the quickest way of shutting Mrs Fraser up was to agree meekly. It wasn't that I was worrying so much about Granny, she had the social worker and the neighbours, but I couldn't help but think I might not see her again. She was eighty-three after all, and though she was tough as her old boots in some ways, she couldn't last for ever. I sighed. But there was nothing I could do. I had to go back to Glasgow.

Glasgow's a city that takes a bit of getting used to. I mean, it wouldn't bowl you over at first sight. It's big, industrial, noisy, and a bit dirty I suppose, but there are green bits too, and the river, and the spires standing up into the sky. I felt as if I was seeing it for the first time as we drove through the streets. I felt as if I was seeing it through James' and Catriona's eyes. And all I could see were grimy tenements, some half-demolished with their sides hanging open, and hardly a trace of green anywhere. Catriona didn't look as if she would much fancy having to live here.

"There's good parts too," I said. "The Botanic Gardens are lovely. . . " Then I shut up. I was sounding like some stupid telly ad, and I didn't have to defend my city anyway.

"Of course," said Mr Fraser heartily. "I'm rather fond of Glasgow myself. The people are very friendly."

Good old Mr Fraser! I could always rely on him to jump in, though sometimes when he did I felt about three years old, needing to be humoured.

I directed him to my street. My tummy was birling a bit. We passed Isobel standing on the corner talking to a boy she was keen on. I waved to her; she stared back, not recognising me in a strange car squashed in amongst strange people. Or perhaps I had undergone a transformation during the summer! When I caught sight of myself in the driving mirror I thought I didn't look much different, only browner. Wait till my mother saw me!

I sneaked a look at James. I'd been trying not to look at him on the journey. The sight of him didn't help my insides. His face was all serious and sober, as if he was going to a funeral. I'd have liked to make a joke but I felt as if my throat would crack if I tried.

"Over there," I directed Mr Fraser. "By the lamp-post."

A crowd of kids scattered to make way for the car. They stood on the pavement to see who would get out. "It's only Maggie McKinley," said one little scruff who lived in the next stair to me. Only Maggie McKinley indeed! I gave him a look that should have squashed him but didn't. Catriona craned her neck to look up at the tenements. A few weeks ago I'd have been hot and bothered at the idea of the Frasers coming to see where I lived. Snob, McKinley! But I wasn't bothered now. Suddenly I realised that I'd never asked James what kind of a house he lived in. In fact I realised that there were a lot of things I'd never asked him, and wanted to. I supposed they lived in a house, not a flat, or maybe a bungalow, with a neat garden in front kept in trim by Mrs Fraser. My mother's always talking about how nice it would be to have a wee bungalow in Bearsden (that's a posh suburb) but she'd go daft in a place like that. Maybe when we're all gone, to explore the Amazon, or whatever, Sandy and Jean and I, then she might get one, so she says. My dad goes on reading the paper and letting her talk. Talk costs nothing, he says.

But it was funny to think of James going off to live in a place I couldn't even picture. We had exchanged addresses and he had said he would write to me every day. I hadn't made any wild promises because I knew myself too well: some days I would write twenty pages, and others I wouldn't write at all.

James and his father got out to help me unload my gear. The kids gawped, trying to see what I had inside all the bags.

"Got everything now, Maggie?" asked Mr Fraser. I nodded. He held out his hand for me to take. "Good-bye then. We'll see you soon, eh? You'll come and visit us?"

"Yes." I felt kind of strangled. It was silly of me. They were only going to be living forty miles away. But it wasn't just the distance. "Thank you," I said. "Thank you very much. For everything."

He said it was a pleasure and he smiled, and got into the car. I said good-bye to Mrs Fraser and Catriona, then looked round at James.

"I'll help you up with your things," he said.

"No, no," I protested. "You don't have to."

"Of course I don't have to. But I want to."

I pushed open the stair door with my foot and we went into the passage that leads to the stairs. It was nearly dark—it always is, except at night when the lights are on—and James stumbled on an uneven bit of the floor.

"Are you all right?"

"Of course."

I dropped my bags. "Don't come all the way up. Please!"

"O.K." He put down the suitcases.

"Say good-bye to me quickly."

He kissed me. We didn't actually say good-bye. He turned and went, light flooded the passage for a moment whilst the door was open, and then I was in the dark again, alone. I heard the Frasers' car engine revving up, and the sound of it driving away.

The stairs were shadowy and smelt strange to me after the long time away. The smells weren't all that great, a mixture of dampness, cat and old stone. I couldn't help thinking of the smell of the pines in the glen. Ah give over, McKinley! You'll get used to it again, and aren't you glad to be home?

I was. I dashed up the stairs, dropping luggage on every side, but not caring or stopping, for I could pick it up later. I couldn't wait now to see my mum and dad and Sandy and Jean.

I opened the front door. "It's me!"

"In here," called my mother.

They were all in the kitchen drinking tea and looking as if someone had stolen the last bun off the plate.

"Greetings, ravers! What's going on here? Having a party?"

"Hi, Maggie," said Jean. "Had a good time?"

"Great. I hope you're all mad with delight to see me?"

Sarcasm's wasted on my family. They just never let on they've heard you. Sandy grunted, my dad nodded so that I would know he'd seen me, and my mum took the cigarette out of her mouth long enough to kiss me.

"You're no looking too bad," she said.

"Thanks."

"I didn't think you were coming home till tomorrow. How's your granny?"

"Fine."

"She's a tough one." My mother turned to my father. "She'll see us all out yet, I'm telling you."

"Must be all that fresh air," I said. "You should have stayed up there, Dad. We could all go back. Return to your family seat!"

My mother gave me one of those withering looks that means Maggie's off her head again. I showed her and Jean the Cairngorm brooch and they thought it was lovely but when I started to tell them about Margaret and Agnes Ross they weren't interested. History's not in their line.

"What *is* the matter with the lot of you?" I demanded. "You look like a lot of drookit hens."

"We've had bad news," said my mother.

My heart leapt. But no, it couldn't be Granny, of course not. But what other kind of bad news was there?

"We're getting pulled down," said my father. He nodded at an official-looking envelope on the sideboard.

"Pulled down? Do you mean—?"

"Aye, cleared out. Put out of our home."

"But we can't," I cried.

"Of course we can," snapped my mother, lighting another cigarette from the butt of her old one. She was all on edge, understandably.

Now we'd known for a long time that it might happen, there had been talk, and rumours, but half of them had contradicted the other, and no one had known anything for sure. The tenements in our street were in good condition, they didn't have to be knocked down because they were slums or anything like that, and everybody had said they weren't going to develop on our side of the road. Now I wondered who 'everybody' was. After a bit the rumours had died down and we'd put it out of our heads.

"Is it certain?" I asked, not needing an answer.

"We're to get rehoused in one of those high blocks,"

said Sandy. "Miles out," he added with disgust. He likes the middle of the town.

"They say they're awful nice inside," said Jean. "My friend Norma—"

I turned on her. "I don't care how nice they are. I don't want to go." She looked hurt, it was a shame, for I didn't mean to sound off at her. Whenever anything bad happens she always finds something nice about it. You know the silver lining thing. Not like me at all. I rage, I don't want to find anything good.

I raged then. "The cheek of them! They think they can treat us like puppets. Move us around and jiggle the strings and we're not even supposed to say boo!" I laid off as if the whole of the town council was in the kitchen. It was a pity they weren't: it might have been good for them, instead of sitting in some office in the City Chambers deciding to put people out of their houses and make them live in places they don't want to live in. What kind of democracy was that? We'd had a debate about it in school and the teacher had said that I didn't think enough about the good of the community as a whole. I wished I'd had him there too. I didn't want to live in one of those concrete slabs and go up and down in a lift with a bunch of strangers. I wanted to stay here, where I was born. Why shouldn't I? My mother and father sat and nodded, agreeing with every word I said.

"You've a good way of putting things, Maggie," said my mother.

"We ought to get her on the council," said Sandy and giggled, as if the idea was totally ludicrous. I glared at him. One day I'd show him. Margaret McKinley, Member of Parliament for . . . No, on second thoughts, I still preferred the Amazon. You wouldn't be able to wear jeans in the House of Commons for a start.

"There's nothing we can do," said Jean.

"You're right," said my father. "They have us over a barrel."

"I shall refuse to move," I declared. "We can all refuse. We can stage a sit-in. Get the neighbours to do the same. I'm sure old Mr Flanagan won't open his door anyway. He never does. And Mrs Slattery's game for anything." I was getting quite excited by the idea. I could see us sitting with arms folded, defying the bull-dozers.

"They'd cut off the water, and the electricity," said my father, whose practical side always gets in the way of ideals.

"Have a cup of tea, Maggie," said my mother, "It'll do you good. And sit down, for goodness' sake. You must be tired after coming all that way."

To her, Inverness-shire is as good as the moon. She speaks about it with the same kind of disbelief, as if it is a fantasy place. She blames all my father's bad habits on being brought up in the back-of-beyond.

I took a cup of tea and subsided into an armchair beside the fire. There must be a way! We didn't have to give in that easily. The Ross women had at least put up a fight. But I could see I'd have a job getting my mother and Jean to cover their heads with red shawls and block the road.

"They're clearing the whole area," sighed my father. "The city's disappearing."

My rage had gone now, and I was engulfed by misery. I liked the street, I knew everyone in it, I hated the sight of those high towers. It wasn't fair!

Life's not fair, lassie, that's what my granny would say; you have to get used to it and make the most of it. It was uncanny: it was almost as if I could hear her voice beside me. I looked round but she wasn't there of course.

She had made the most of having to move, and so had Margaret Ross, once she saw there was nothing else to be done. I wasn't going to have to tramp over moors and hills to find a new home, though in a way I'd have fancied that more. But that was just me being romantic and forgetting her misery. I put my hand over the brooch. If my granny and her granny could do it, then so could I!

"I suppose we'll just have to make the best of it, won't we?" I said.

"You've changed your tune quickly," said my mother.

I shrugged.

"She aye makes a noise to start with," said my father. "And then she sees reason. You know what she's like."

"Thank you," I said, with heavy sarcasm.

"I could be doing with another cup of tea," he said.

Jean got up and poured it.

"It might not be so bad," I said. "If we got right up at the top. I'd fancy that. Then we could look down and see the whole city."

It might be like being up on the mountain looking down on the glen. Well, just a bit.

ALSO IN

HEINEMANN
NEW WINDMILLS

General Editors: Anne and Ian Serraillier

Chinua Achebe Things Fall Apart
Vivien Alcock The Cuckoo Sister; The Monster Garden
Michael Anthony Green Days by the River
Bernard Ashley High Pavement Blues; Running Scared
J. G. Ballard Empire of the Sun
Martin Ballard Dockie
Stan Barstow Joby
Nina Bawden On the Run; The Witch's Daughter; A Handful of
Thieves; Carrie's War; The Robbers; Devil by the Sea; Kept in the
Dark; The Finding
Judy Blume It's Not the End of the World; Tiger Eyes
E R Braithwaite To Sir, With Love
F Hodgson Burnett The Secret Garden
Betsy Byars The Midnight Fox
Victor Canning The Runaways; Flight of the Grey Goose
John Christopher The Guardians; Empty World
Jane Leslie Conly Racso and the Rats of NIMH
Roald Dahl Danny, The Champion of the World; The Wonderful
Story of Henry Sugar; George's Marvellous Medicine; The BFG;
The Witches; Boy; Going Solo; Charlie and the Chocolate Factory
Andrew Davies Conrad's War
Anita Desai The Village by the Sea
Peter Dickinson The Gift; Annerton Pit; Healer
Berlie Doherty Granny was a Buffer Girl
J M Falkner Moonfleet
Anne Fine The Granny Project
F Scott Fitzgerald The Great Gatsby
Leon Garfield Six Apprentices
Kenneth Grahame The Wind in the Willows
Graham Greene The Third Man and The Fallen Idol; The Power
and the Glory; Brighton Rock
Thomas Hardy The Withered Arm and Other Wessex Tales

Rosemary Harris Zed
L P Hartley The Go-Between
Esther Hautzig The Endless Steppe
Ernest Hemingway The Old Man and the Sea; A Farewell to Arms
Nat Hentoff Does this School have Capital Punishment?
Nigel Hinton Getting Free; Buddy; Buddy's Song
Minfong Ho Rice Without Rain
Geoffrey Household Rogue Male
Janni Howker Badger on the Barge; Isaac Campion
Monica Hughes Ring-Rise, Ring-Set
Shirley Hughes Here Comes Charlie Moon
Kristin Hunter Soul Brothers and Sister Lou
Barbara Ireson (Editor) in a Class of Their Own
Jennifer Johnston Shadows on Our Skin
Toeckey Jones Go Well, Stay Well
James Joyce A Portrait of the Artist as a Young Man
Erich Kästner Emil and the Detectives
Geraldine Kaye Comfort Herself
Clive King Me and My Million
Dick King-Smith The Sheep-Pig
Daniel Keyes Flowers for Algernon
D H Lawrence The Fox and The Virgin and the Gypsy; Selected Tales
Harper Lee To Kill a Mockingbird
Laurie Lee As I Walked Out One Midsummer Morning
Julius Lester Basketball Game
Ursula Le Guin A Wizard of Earthsea
C Day Lewis The Otterbury Incident
David Line Run for Your Life; Screaming High
Joan Lingard Across the Barricades; Into Exile; The Clearance; The File on Fraulein Berg
Penelope Lively The Ghost of Thomas Kempe
Jack London The Call of the Wild; White Fang
Bernard Mac Laverty Cal
Margaret Mahy The Haunting; The Catalogue of The Universe
Jan Mark Thunder and Lightning; Under the Autumn Garden

How many have you read?